JOHN WILSON

LOST CAUSE

DISCARD

ORCA BOOK PUBLISHERS

Library and Archives Canada Cataloguing in Publication

Wilson, John (John Alexander), 1951-
Lost cause / John Wilson.
(Seven (the series))

Issued also in an electronic format.
ISBN 978-1-55469-944-5

I. Title. II. Series: Seven the series
PS8595.I5834L66 2012   jC813'.54   C2012-902619-0

First published in the United States, 2012
Library of Congress Control Number: 2012938224

Summary: Steve travels to Spain and uncovers his late grandfather's
involvement in the Spanish Civil War.

*Orca Book Publishers is dedicated to preserving the environment and has
printed this book on Forest Stewardship Council® certified paper.*

Orca Book Publishers gratefully acknowledges the support for its publishing
programs provided by the following agencies: the Government of Canada
through the Canada Book Fund and the Canada Council for the Arts,
and the Province of British Columbia through the BC Arts Council
and the Book Publishing Tax Credit.

Design by Teresa Bubela
Cover photography by Getty Images
Author photo by Katherine Gordon

ORCA BOOK PUBLISHERS
PO Box 5626, Stn. B
Victoria, BC Canada
V8R 6S4

ORCA BOOK PUBLISHERS
PO Box 468
Custer, WA USA
98240-0468

www.orcabook.com
Printed and bound in Canada.

15 14 13 12 • 5 4 3 2

A story for Jake, Darcy and Ebony.

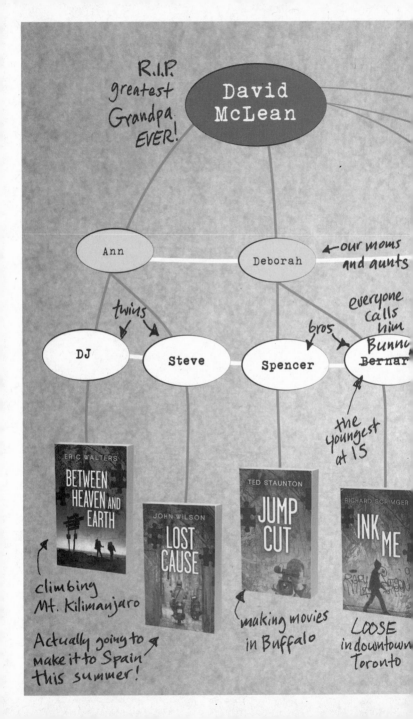

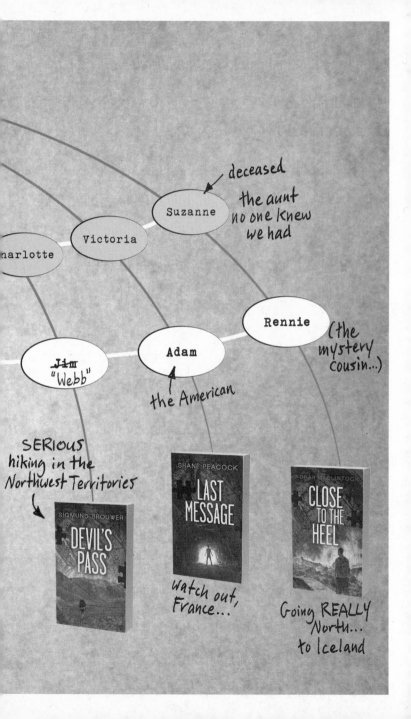

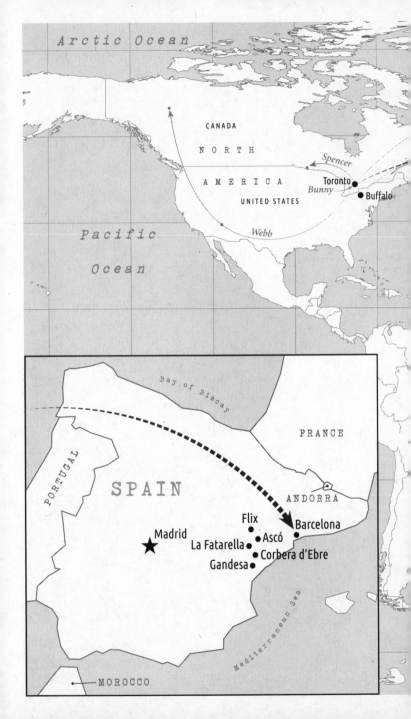

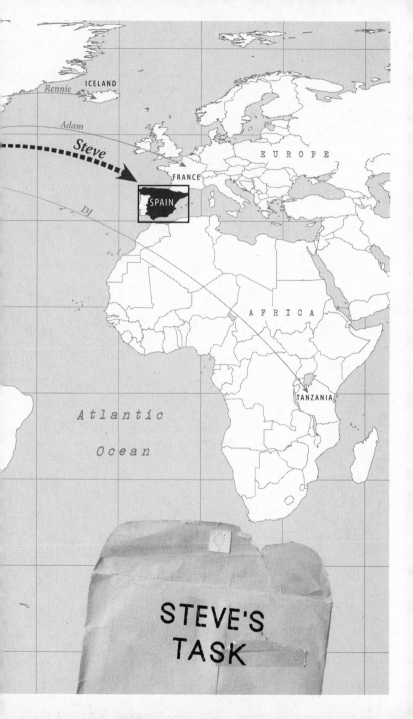

ONE

"I don't see why I have to go," I said. I spoke quietly, forcing my voice to be calm and trying not to upset my mother. "The funeral, yes. I went to that so that the whole family could be together, but this is just some lawyer reading the will. There's not going to be anything in it that affects me. I can't see why they couldn't just send the will out or email it."

The whole idea struck me as so old-fashioned—everyone gathered in a dusty room like in the climax of one of Agatha Christie's Hercule Poirot mysteries. Not that I didn't enjoy mysteries. In fact I loved them, from the Encyclopedia Brown and Hardy Boys books when I was a kid to the more complex stories I read now by Ian Rankin and Robert Wilson. Trouble was, this sounded like it was going to be less of a mystery and more of a really boring afternoon.

Actually, I wasn't as dead set against going to the will reading as I must have sounded to Mom. It was just that I had spent the days after my grandfather's death ignoring what I wanted to do and doing what everyone else wanted. I felt totally overwhelmed. It was like I was drowning in this tsunami of raw emotion, and I needed a break.

I didn't dislike my grandfather, although as a little kid I had been scared of the gruff old man who had that old-person smell. I simply didn't share everyone else's hero worship of him. Oh, he was nice enough, always gave us good gifts on birthdays and at Christmas, tried to attend our school plays and sports events. He had done interesting things, like being a pilot in the war and all, but lots of people did stuff like that. I suppose the problem was not with Grandfather but with the way other people built him up out of all proportion.

My brother DJ, for example. At the funeral, he had stood up and made a long tearful speech about how wonderful Grandfather was and all the incredible things he had done in his life. As if DJ knew what the old guy had done decades before he was even born. I wanted my own life back, and I really couldn't see the point of going to the will reading.

The problem was that I was being rational and reasonable, but Mom made it personal. "Steven, I know Dad and you didn't see eye to eye, but I'd like you to come along, for me."

I knew then that I'd lost the argument. For a start, my name's Steve. Every time Mom calls me Steven, I feel like I'm five years old again. And playing the "do it for me" card was the clincher. Mom had been an emotional wreck these past few days. She was continually red-eyed, and I had heard her walking around the house in the middle of the night—a sure sign that she was upset and couldn't sleep. How was I supposed to turn her down?

"Okay," I said, swallowing the urge to argue. "I'll come, for you."

"Thank you," she said. "I wish you had got to know him better. He really was an extraordinary man."

"I've got to go, Mom," I said hurriedly, before she launched into another recitation of all the wonderful things my grandfather had done. "I really need to update my résumé if I'm going to get a job that pays enough for me to go to Europe this summer." I thought but didn't say, *And lets me get away from the family for a few weeks.*

"All right, dear," Mom said, leaning over and kissing me on the forehead. I disappeared upstairs as fast as my legs could carry me.

For ten minutes, I stared at my résumé on the computer screen. It didn't belong to someone on the fast track for a Nobel Prize or a career as the CEO of IBM. A summer working at McDonald's last year, a couple of years getting up at the crack of dawn for a paper route, a few weeks here and there stacking boxes at the local grocery store and, if I stretched back far enough, playing Lego and video games with the kid down the road while his parents escaped to a movie. All for minimum wage.

I had $932.78 saved. Almost enough for the airfare to Europe if I was lucky, but I was going to get awfully bored if I couldn't afford to leave London airport and really hungry if I didn't eat for three or four weeks. I needed a high-paying job and I needed it fast; otherwise, my dream of traveling in Europe was looking more and more like a lost cause, at least for this year.

I think the obvious impossibility of what I was trying to do was the only reason Mom wasn't freaking out about my plan to go to Europe on my own at age seventeen. "Next year will be here before you know it," she said. "Save up this summer. We can still have a break, up at Dad's cabin on the lake for a week or two." Her voice caught when she said this, but she recovered. "You and DJ and I can have a nice family holiday."

Even with a suitcase full of mystery novels and my laptop, the thought of two weeks trapped in a cabin with Mom and my twin brother DJ as an alternative to seeing Europe sent shivers down my spine. But what choice did I have? Short of winning the lottery, which would be tough since I wasn't even old enough to buy a ticket, it looked like this year's holiday would be spent being fussed over by Mom, arguing with DJ and swatting mosquitoes on the shores of Lake Moose Droppings.

With his usual impeccable timing, DJ, my always-right, football-playing jock of a twin brother, knocked on my door and, without waiting for a reply, barged in. "Hi, little brother," he said cheerfully. DJ was born fifteen minutes before me. Now, this is hardly grounds for him being my big brother, but I've been his little brother as long as I can remember. Add to that his relentless optimism and belief that everything is simple and will work out for the best, and my nerves frequently stretch past breaking point.

"What, bro?" I asked. I call him bro because he once asked me not to. I figured it annoyed him, although he showed no sign that it did. But there was no way I was going to call him big brother.

"Mom says you don't want to come to the will reading," he said, completely ignoring the exasperation in my voice and my attempt to aggravate him. He plopped himself down on the edge of my bed. "I'm glad you changed your mind. The family needs to be together at a time like this. Everyone should go to the will reading to show respect to Grandpa."

I resisted the temptation to point out that Grandfather was past caring who went to the reading of his will, and said instead, "We all went to the funeral, the whole family and dozens of friends. That showed respect. This is just a lawyer's thing. The will was probably written years ago anyway."

"Some of Grandpa's money will come to Mom and that'll help." DJ's voice was taking on the preachy tone he used when he was explaining something that he thought I was too dense to understand. "She's been working long hours to keep this family together, and she's very stressed. It's been really hard for her with Dad dying when we were both so young."

"I know that," I said, my voice rising despite my attempt to keep it under control. "I'm not stupid."

DJ looked at me with that half-smile of his that seemed to say, *It's all right. When you're as old and smart as I am, you'll understand.* "You could help out more around the house." DJ scanned my room. "Clean up this pit for a start. I bet there's a whole ecosystem evolving under that pile of soccer stuff in the corner."

"My room is my space," I said, swallowing hard. "Mom agreed we were in charge of our own space, and just because you want to live in a compulsively tidy, antiseptic cell, doesn't mean everyone else has to."

DJ nodded infuriatingly and changed the subject before I could get any angrier. "You still planning on Europe this summer?"

It took me a moment to adjust to the new topic. "Yeah, if I can get enough money together."

"You think traveling alone's such a good idea?"

Here we go again, I thought. A gentle reminder from my older and wiser brother that I might be about to make a mistake. "I can handle it, bro," I said. "Besides, I might not be alone. Sam has relatives over there, and he might be visiting them this summer. We've talked about hanging out together."

"Is Sam the nerdy English kid with the curly hair who spends his time building model planes?"

"So what?" I said, challenging DJ to criticize some more, but he simply shrugged. "What are *you* planning to do this summer that's so hot?"

"I don't know," DJ said. "Work, put some money aside for college. Mom's talking about going up to Grandpa's cabin. That'll be a good time."

"Yippee," I said with as much sarcasm in my voice as I could muster. "Look, if I'm going to Europe, I need to get a job, so I have to get my résumé in order." I turned back to my computer screen.

DJ stood and took a couple of steps toward the door. Then he stopped, turned and said, "I'd come with you to Europe, you know. If I could." Then he was gone.

I sat back and stared at the ceiling. That was typical of DJ. Assuming I couldn't manage on my own. Trying to "big brother" me. It got on my nerves. On the other hand, I appreciated that he would do whatever he could to make my dream possible. His superior attitude bugged me like crazy, but we *were* twins. Deep down, we both knew that if the other got in trouble, we would do whatever it took to help.

Why did life have to be so complicated? I sighed and looked back at my computer screen. The more immediate question was, how was I going to make flipping burgers for three months seem like the perfect qualification for a twenty-buck-an-hour job?

TWO

"Good afternoon," the lawyer said as he settled himself behind the largest desk I had ever seen. The eleven other people in the room mumbled a response. I remained silent.

The room was big, but it still felt stuffy with so many people in it. The walls were paneled in dark wood, and the one behind the desk was a solid mass of glass-fronted bookcases filled with regimented rows of identical legal books. It looked as if the place had been arranged by DJ at his most compulsively neat.

The six adults—Mom, her three sisters and two of my uncles—sat on a huge, overstuffed leather couch and a loveseat in front of the lawyer's desk. DJ and two of my cousins, Spencer and Webb, sat in three similar armchairs. My other cousins, Bunny and Adam, perched on the wide arms of one of the chairs. I stood at the back. Before the lawyer came in, Mom had looked up at me and patted the arm of the sofa beside her, but I had shaken my head. I was here, but I didn't have to be part of the proceedings. A shiny black, flat-screen TV sat in a cabinet to one side as if it was watching us all.

The lawyer was talking, thanking us for coming, making some minor asides to put us at ease and saying what a wonderful man Grandfather had been, but I wasn't listening. I was thinking I could probably live comfortably for a week in Europe on what the lawyer's suit cost.

Now he was going on about selling assets and splitting the money between Mom and her sisters. That was good. Mom deserved a break. The cottage was to be kept and shared among us all. Great, I thought, that really is where I'm going to spend the summer. Then he said something that caught my attention.

"This is without a doubt one of the most unusual clauses that I have ever been asked to put in a will."

I wasn't the only one interested. The lawyer was slowly scanning the room, and everyone was staring back at him like mice mesmerized by a snake.

"I know you are all anxious to hear about these undertakings," the lawyer continued. "However, I cannot share them with all of you." A burst of protest came from several relatives, but he raised his hands. "Please, please! You will all be fully informed, but not all of you will be informed at the same time. Some people will have to leave the room prior to the undertakings being read."

"Wonderful," I murmured under my breath. "All the fuss about coming, and I'm going to be sent out with the other kids."

"Therefore," the lawyer went on, "as per the terms of the will, I request that the grandsons—"

"I'm not going anywhere," I blurted out. Everyone turned to stare at me. I hadn't meant to say anything out loud, it just kind of escaped. Since I had been forced to come here, I wanted to stay for the only bit that promised to be remotely inter-esting. "I don't want to be kicked out of the room," I concluded weakly.

"You'll go if you're told to go." Trust DJ to butt in. He probably felt I was embarrassing the family. Same old, same old.

"You don't understand." The lawyer looked at DJ. "He *can* stay."

"If he's staying, then I'm staying as well," DJ said.

"Me too," Webb pitched in, and a babble of voices erupted around the room.

The lawyer stood up. "Could everybody please just stop," he said in a voice that any of my teachers would have been proud of. "Please, I am reading a will. Decorum is needed. Out of respect for the deceased, you all need to follow his directions. Is that understood?"

Everyone fell silent. "Sorry," DJ said.

"Me too," I added sheepishly.

"Before I go on, I need to ask *everybody*"—he looked hard across the room at me—"to agree to respect the terms of his will—*all* the terms of his will."

I nodded; so did everyone else. "Of course we agree," my mother said.

"Excellent." The lawyer sat back down. "Now, I need everyone except the six grandsons to leave the room."

Now it was the adults' turn to blurt out objections.

"What?" Charlotte, Webb's mother, asked.

"Did you say all the adults have to leave?" Aunt Debbie added.

"Yes." The lawyer nodded. "Everyone except the grandsons."

A broad grin spread across my face as the adults filed out in confusion. I had been dumb to blurt out my complaint based on a wrong assumption, but my aunts and uncles had been no better. They had stayed quiet only because they had made the same assumption as me. When that turned out to be wrong, they had blurted out their complaints just as I had.

My mother was the last adult to leave the room. As she left, she smiled back at DJ and closed the door. My cousins spread out into the vacant seats. I stayed standing at the back.

"Well, gentlemen," the lawyer said, clasping his hands beneath his chin. "I am assuming that nobody saw this coming."

"Grandpa was always full of surprises," Bunny said.

"So," I said, feeling more comfortable now that the adults had left, "I guess because of that we're *not* that surprised."

"Interesting perspective," the lawyer said. "The only way you would have been surprised is if he didn't do something to surprise you."

"Pretty much," I said.

"So if he'd done nothing then you would have actually been surprised, which wouldn't have been a surprise. Sort of a Catch-22, don't you think?"

"Do you think, sir, that we could go on?" DJ said. I flashed him a vicious glare for being so pompous, but he ignored me. "I believe we're all anxious to hear what you're going to tell us."

"I'm sure you are," the lawyer said. "But, actually, *I'm* not going to tell you anything. Your *grandfather* is."

Everyone tensed at that, and I caught DJ glancing toward the door as if he expected Grandfather to walk through it.

"I'm going to play a video your grandfather made." The lawyer picked up a remote and pointed it at the shiny black TV. "I was in the room when your grandfather recorded this." He pressed a button and the TV flickered into life. "I think *all* of you will be at least a little surprised by what he has to say." He pressed a second button, and Grandfather appeared on the screen.

I watched, enthralled. We all did. I know I had never felt particularly close to Grandfather, but it was weird seeing and hearing him almost from beyond the grave.

"I'm not sure why I have to be wearing makeup," he said to someone off camera. "This is my will, not some late-night talk show...and it's certainly not a *live* taping." The figure off camera laughed, and I found myself smiling. That was the sort of black humor I enjoyed.

"Good morning...or afternoon, boys," he began, turning to face the camera and us. "If you're watching this, I must be dead, although on this fine afternoon I feel very much alive." Grandfather looked exactly as I remembered him, wearing his trademark black beret and the sweater I remembered Mom knitting him a couple of winters ago.

"I want to start off by saying that I don't want you to be sad. I had a good life and I wouldn't change a minute of it. That said, I still hope that you are at least a little sad and that you miss having me around. After all, I was one *spectacular* grandpa!"

A chuckle rose from the group, and I had to admit that I did miss him, now that I could only see him on TV.

"And you were simply the best grandsons a man could ever have. I want you to know that of all the joys in my life, you were among my greatest. From the first time I met each of you to the last moments I spent with you"—Grandfather smiled slightly—"and of course I don't know what those last moments were, but I know they were wonderful, I want to thank you all for being part of my life. A very big, special, wonderful, warm part of my life."

It was soppy and sentimental. I knew that, but it didn't stop a tear forming in the corner of my eye as I watched the old man reach forward and take a sip of water from the glass on the desk in front of him. His hand shook ever so slightly. Was he nervous? He never struck me as someone who felt fear.

"I wanted to record this rather than have my lawyer read it out to you." A smile turned the corners of my grandfather's lips up. "Hello, Johnnie."

"Hello, Davie," the lawyer replied with a matching smile.

Grandfather glanced off screen. "I hope you appreciate that twenty-year-old bottle of Scotch I left you. And you better not have had more than one snort of it before the reading of my will." He looked back at us and winked.

The lawyer held up two fingers.

"But knowing you the way I do, I suspect you would have had two."

The lawyer looked embarrassed. "He did know me well."

I shook my head to try and get rid of the feeling of weirdness. Here was my dead grandfather talking to us and his lawyer in this room and also to the same lawyer who was at the recording of the message. It was eerie.

"I just thought I wanted—needed—to say goodbye to all of you in person. Or at least as in person as this allows.

"Life is an interesting journey, one that seldom takes you where you think you might be going. Certainly, I never expected that I was going to ever become an old man. In fact, there were more than a few times when I was a boy that I didn't believe I was going to live to see another day, never mind live long enough to grow old.

"But I did live a long and wonderful life. I was blessed to meet the love of my life, your grandmother Vera. It's so sad that she passed on before any of you had a chance to meet her. I know people never speak ill of the dead—and I'm counting on you all to keep up that tradition with me—but your grandmother was simply the most perfect woman in the world. Her only flaw, as far as I can see, was being foolish enough to marry me."

As Grandfather talked on about how proud he was of his daughters—our mothers—and how he had loved coming to all our school plays and soccer games, my mind began to wander. Something he'd said in the video was nagging at me. My brow furrowed in concentration. He'd often talked about his time as a pilot in the Second World War, but I'd never heard him refer to almost dying as a boy. What did it all mean? I didn't know any stories from before his time as a pilot. What had he done when he was younger that made him think he was going to die? It was a mystery.

The flickering image on the screen drew me back to Grandfather and his story. Mom had guilted me into coming today, but wild horses couldn't have dragged me away now.

Grandfather was finishing off his account of how much joy we had brought him. "You boys, you wonderful, incredible, lovely boys, have been such a blessing…seven blessings…"

Out of the corner of my eye I noticed DJ tense up. Then I realized why. There were six grandsons, not seven. Was the old man's brain not as sharp as he thought? His voice caught and he covered it by taking a long sip of water.

"But I didn't bring you here simply to tell you how much I loved you all," he went on eventually. "Being part of your lives was one of the greatest achievements of my life, and I wouldn't trade it for anything, but being there for all your big moments meant that I couldn't be elsewhere. I've done a lot, but it doesn't seem that time is going to permit me the luxury of doing everything I wished for. So, I have some requests, some *last* requests."

The six of us looked at each other, but everyone was as confused as I was.

"In the possession of my lawyer are some envelopes. One for each of you."

Six heads swung around, as if programmed, to look at the lawyer. He smiled and waved a fan of manila envelopes at us.

Grandfather reclaimed our attention. "Each of these requests, these tasks, has been specifically selected for you to fulfill. All of the things you will need to complete your task will be provided—money, tickets, guides. Everything.

"I am not asking any of you to do anything stupid or unnecessarily reckless—certainly nothing as stupid or reckless as I did at your ages."

There it was again, a reference to mysterious things he had done as a boy. What was going on?

"Your parents may be worried, but I have no doubts. Just as I have no doubts that you will all become fine young men. I am sad that I will not be there to watch you all grow into the incredible men I know you will become. But I don't need to be there to know that will happen. I am so certain of that. As certain as I am that I will be there with you as you complete my last requests, as you continue your life journeys."

The air in the room felt heavy with silence. We were barely breathing. Grandfather lifted his glass. "A final toast," he said, "to the best grandsons a man could ever have." He tipped back the glass, drained it, replaced it on the table and stared at us. "I love you all so much. Good luck."

The screen went black, and we all let out the breath we hadn't realized we had been holding. The lawyer switched off the TV. "In my hands are the seven envelopes. One for each grandson."

"You mean six." DJ spoke the thought that was in all our minds. "There are only six of us."

"Well," the lawyer said, a slight smile playing around his eyes, "as I said, there is a most interesting twist. There *is* a seventh grandson."

❉

After the adults filed back in, stared at us oddly and settled themselves, the lawyer explained to them what had gone on and replayed Grandfather's DVD. My mom and her sisters were sobbing by the end. The lawyer gave them a moment to calm down, and then he'd repeated the bombshell about the seventh grandson.

It didn't come as such a shock for Mom and the others. Grandfather had told them that they had an unknown half sister and another nephew. He had also asked them to keep it from us boys.

Apparently, Grandfather had been quite the lad, and the result had been a fifth daughter named Suzanne, who had then had a son called Rennie Charbonneau. This kid was the same age as DJ and me, but Grandfather had only discovered his existence a few months ago from reading an obituary in the newspaper.

I couldn't help smiling as I wondered how many cousins or half cousins I might have scattered across the world. This meeting had definitely been worth coming to. It had given me a much greater sense of Grandfather as a person, and it had also given me a quest and a real mystery to solve. I looked down at the envelope in my hand.

"Aren't you going to open it?" Mom was standing beside me.

I shook my head. "I'll wait till I get home."

I looked around the room. The meeting appeared to have broken up. DJ was standing looking at his envelope, and several of my cousins were in huddles with their parents, talking quietly. I hefted *my* envelope. It was light, not much in it. I was eager to know what my task was, but I was also enjoying the anticipation, the not knowing, the mystery. Grandfather had mentioned tickets, money and guides. Perhaps my summer wasn't going to be as disappointing and boring as I had thought.

Steve,

I hope you came to the will reading and are examining the contents of this envelope with an open mind. I know we have not always seen eye to eye. We are, after all, separated by two generations and the world I grew up in was very different from the one that you know. I hope that this will not be a handicap to our friendship, even if that friendship will be a bit one-sided now!

Rosa Luxemburg, a heroine of mine when I was your age, once said something to the effect that freedom only meant something if it was freedom for those who think differently. I think something similar applies to friendship.

Being friends with those who are the same as you, have the same interests and beliefs, is easy. The problem is that you miss much of the richness that makes us human. Seek out the odd and unusual, the novel ideas of those who think differently from you.

Sorry, I seem to be preaching. I don't mean to, it's just that I wanted my letter to you to be as long as the ones to your brother and your cousins. This letter will be short for two reasons.

1) I know how much you dislike sentimental stuff, so I won't go into any details about how cute you were when you and your brother first came into this world! I suspect that, deep down, you are as sentimental as the rest of us, but that you keep it hidden. Probably a good characteristic when you become a scientist, which seem to me to be where your interests lie.

2) Your task is very simply explained, although it may not be as easy as you imagine to carry out. I could certainly give you more information and point you in certain directions, but this is your task, not mine. You must find your own way, make your own decisions and come to your own conclusions. I know how much you love mystery novels, so I am going to give you a real-life mystery to solve.

Some time ago, a letter from Spain came for me. It had found me through an organization of which I am a member. It was from someone I had known many years before, and it had been mailed from an address I hadn't thought about in more than seven decades.

The address was from a time in my life that was full of importance, danger, love and a sense of being a part of something that would change the world. Of course, the world didn't change, at least not in the way that I hoped, but that time was so important to me that I sometimes think I have spent my life since then trying to recapture it.

That is your task, to recapture that time. I can't tell you how to do it. All I can do is give you clues to set you on a path that, I hope, will solve the mystery of the letter. I gave you a clue in the DVD, and to that I can add the address where the letter came from. I will not show you the letter itself; it contained a lot of personal stuff that would be of little interest to you, but it did say that there was something of mine at that address. At first, I intended to go to the address myself, but I delayed. I suppose I'm frightened to go back to that time when life was so vibrant that I almost thought I would explode with the passion of it all. In fact, it was such an intense time that I have never talked about it with anyone. If you discover what I think you will, you will be the only person who knows about this part of my life.

I have instructed my lawyer, Johnnie, to mail a letter to the address, informing them of my demise and of your arrival. They cannot get in touch with you except through Johnnie, and without solving the mystery, what would you say to them in a letter? Suffice it to say that the people at that address will be expecting you and, I hope, will be your guides on your quest.

Steve, you are young and passion is your preserve, so I pass this task on to you. Solve the mystery and, I hope, discover a little of the passion I felt in those long-ago days.

Good luck and always remember that I love you.

Grandfather

THREE

I read Grandfather's letter through one more time and tipped the contents of the envelope out onto my bed. There was a scrap of paper with two handwritten verses of poetry on it:

> They clung like birds to the long expresses that lurch
> Through unjust lands, through the night, through the
>   alpine tunnel;
> They floated over oceans;
> They walked the passes. All presented their lives.

The stars are dead. The animals will not look.
We are left alone with our day, and time is short, and
History to the defeated
May say Alas but cannot help nor pardon.

A second piece of paper had an address on it:

Maria Dolores Calderon Garcia
Carrer de la Portaferrissa, 71
08002 Barcelona
España

Folded in the second piece of paper was a small tarnished key. It was old-fashioned and too small to be a door key. Nothing written on the paper gave a clue as to its use.

The final two things in the envelope made my heart race. The first was a note from Grandfather telling me that the lawyer had instructions to buy me a return airline ticket to Barcelona. The second was a bank card with my name on it and paperwork showing a balance of $2,000 on the card. All it needed was my signature. Suddenly my lost cause wasn't so lost after all. Europe *was* possible this summer.

I hadn't planned on going to Barcelona, but I hadn't been anywhere in Europe, so one place was as good as another to begin. There were only two problems: the language and Mom. I couldn't speak Spanish. But I liked languages, so I could probably pick up a few key phrases before I went. Mom would be tougher. Would she allow me to head off to a foreign country on my own?

I'd have to cross that bridge when I came to it. Right now I just wanted to savor the possibilities. I took a deep breath. "Thank you, Grandfather," I murmured. I let the documents slip out of my grasp onto the bed beside me. That's when a black-and-white photograph slid out from behind the paperwork.

It was the size of a postcard, faded and grainy. To one side, two figures stood in a doorway beneath an intricately carved lintel. The figures were tough to make out but were obviously a boy and a girl, about my age. He wore heavy boots, gray pants with an open-neck shirt tucked into them, and a short leather jacket. He was bareheaded and his dark hair was thick, parted in the middle and swept back above his ears.

The girl was dressed in what looked like mechanics' overalls. She wore a broad dark scarf tied around her neck and a peaked cap. Her hair was dark, shoulder length and tucked behind her ears. I didn't recognize either of them, but they looked happy. Both were grinning broadly at the camera.

My gaze drifted to the lintel, where a crown sat above a shield bearing nine vertical lines. On each side, carved vegetation spread out and down to surround the doorway.

A wall stretched away to the left, bare except for a crudely painted hammer and sickle and words that were out of focus but looked like *Mac* and *Pap*.

The photograph was obviously old. I turned it over, looking for a date and the identity of the people, but there was only something written in Spanish: *El fascismo será destruido.*

I spread the contents of the envelope in an arc across the bed: the letter, the scrap of poetry, the address, the key, the note about the ticket, the bank card and the photograph. I put the note and the bank card to one side. They were practical things to help me solve the mystery, but they weren't clues. There were five clues. No, six. In the letter Grandfather had said there had been a clue in the DVD.

I closed my eyes and replayed Grandfather's message in my mind. It was a straightforward message to the six—no, seven—of us. Where was the clue? I ran through it once more.

My eyes flew open in sudden realization. The only bit of the DVD that hadn't made sense to me—Grandfather had talked about the times he had thought he was going to die as a boy. I couldn't remember the exact wording, but I did remember wondering what he had done before the war. Could that be the time when the mysterious events had happened?

I picked up the letter and scanned it. There: *an address I hadn't thought about in more than seven decades.* That would put the importance of the address in the late 1930s, *before* the Second World War broke out in 1939. My grandfather's mystery had something to do with Barcelona in the years before the Second World War.

I felt ridiculously happy. I was going to Europe this summer, and I had already made progress on my task. What other clues could I decipher?

I moved over to my desk and pulled out a sheet of paper from the printer. Systematically I went through the items from the envelope, jotting down what I thought might be clues. I put a question mark beside the things I was doubtful about. I put a line through the clues I thought I had already understood.

The letter
    Rosa Luxemburg?
    ~~DVD~~
    ~~More than seven decades ago~~
The poetry fragments
    "They clung like birds"
    "The stars are dead"
The address
    Maria Dolores Calderon Garcia
    Carrer de la Portaferrissa, 71
    08002 Barcelona
    España
The key
    What does it open?
The photograph
    Identity of the people?
    Location and date of the photograph?
    Meaning of the writing on the wall?

I sat back and scanned my list. Even assuming I hadn't missed anything important, it didn't mean much. Still, I had nowhere else to go. I took a second sheet of paper and wrote down what I had worked out so far.

Barcelona
Late 1930s
Dangerous, passionate, dramatic events

It was a short list. I fired up my computer and typed *Rosa Luxemburg* into Google and got nearly two million hits. I quickly discovered that she had been a Communist a hundred years ago and was murdered during a revolution in Berlin in 1919, before my grandfather was even born. I found the quote about freedom that he had mentioned, but what did that mean? Then I remembered something. I checked the photograph. The scrawled hammer and sickle on the wall beside the door was the Communist symbol. Rosa Luxemburg was a Communist. Did *that* mean anything? I wrote *Communist?* on my list and scored through *Rosa Luxemburg*. Now for the poems.

In quotation marks, I typed *"They clung like birds to the long expresses that lurch."* I got thirty-eight hits, all from a poem called *Spain* by someone called W.H. Auden. I typed *"The stars are dead. The animals will not look"* and got one hundred and thirty-three hits, again all from Auden's *Spain*. I found a copy and read the whole long poem. I could make little of it as it jumped from insurance cards and today's struggle to octaves of radiation. Poetry's never been my thing. The only fact that might make sense was that the poem was written in 1937. I added *1937?* to my list and struck out the poetry fragments on the other page, hoping the address would give me more. It did.

Google Maps showed me a narrow, cobbled street in something called the Gothic Quarter of Barcelona. The little yellow man led me past the walls of old buildings with balconies so close together you could spit across the street. Outside number 71 I stopped and rotated. I almost choked. Right in front of me, filling my computer screen, was the doorway in the photograph.

There wasn't anyone standing in the doorway, and the door itself—a heavy, embossed wooden thing—was closed, but there was no mistaking the crown and the shield above it or the carving around it. I stared at it for a long time and then wrote: *Photo taken at Carrer de la Portaferrissa, 71. But when?*

The door. Was this where Maria Dolores Calderon Garcia lived—lives? Was she to be my guide? Was she the girl in the photograph? If so, she must be very old now. As old as my grandfather. Was that him beside her? The timing was about right if the photograph was taken in the late 1930s.

I shook my head. I shouldn't jump to conclusions. I must let the clues lead me to answers, but only when I am sure of the answers. That's what Hercule Poirot would do. I made a mental note to ask Mom if she had any old photographs of Grandfather and moved on.

My search for *"Mac"* yielded millions of results and I didn't even get out of the ones about computers before I got bored. *"Pap"* was little better. The results were more varied and included a test for cancer, the Peoples' Action Party in Singapore and the Pan-African Parliament, but nothing that anyone would write on a wall in Spain back in 1937.

The phrase *El fascismo será destruido* translated from the Spanish as *Fascism will be destroyed*.

A search for the quote in English only led to a bunch of weird sites about the end of global capitalism and the coming apocalypse. I wrote down *Fascism will be destroyed*, but only because my list was looking very short. This was another dead end, another lost cause. There was only one more route I could think of to try at the moment.

I grabbed the photograph and headed for the kitchen, where Mom was preparing spaghetti and meat sauce for supper. "Do you know who this is?" I asked, holding the photograph out.

I thought she was going to drop the ladle. "Where did you get that?" she asked.

"It was in the envelope that Grandfather gave me," I said. "Is it him?"

"Yes," she said. "It's him. He's very young, and I don't know who the girl is or where it was taken."

"It was taken in Barcelona, I think, around 1937 or '38."

"That would make sense. He looks about your age." Mom turned to look at me. "I never realized how much you look like him."

I hadn't either. It was difficult to get past the weird haircut. "Do you know why he was in Spain then?"

Mom shook her head. "I know very little about when he was young. I know he flew in the war, but before that? I don't think he ever spoke about it much."

That would have been too easy, I thought. "Thanks," I said, turning to go back to my room.

"What is it he wants you to do?" Mom asked as I retreated.

I gritted my teeth and slowly turned back. Would Mom let me go? I didn't want to get into it yet. I needed time to figure out how best to present the trip to her. But I couldn't escape now. I had to say something. "Grandfather wants me to go to Spain."

At that moment, DJ came out of his room. He was grinning like his face would crack. "I'm going to climb a mountain in Tanzania," he said.

FOUR

"Family meeting," Mom said.

I groaned. Mom lowered the heat under the spaghetti sauce and ushered DJ and me to the kitchen table.

"Spain? Tanzania?" she asked. "What is going on?"

"It's Grandpa's request," DJ said, sitting down. "He's asked me to scatter his ashes from the top of Mount Kilimanjaro."

"You're going to Africa to climb a mountain on your own?" Mom said. I was glad that DJ had blurted out his task and was now taking the brunt of Mom's concern. "That's insane."

"It's okay," DJ said calmly. He was always better than me at staying unruffled when talking to Mom. "Grandpa has it all organized. I'll fly over on my own, but there's a guide to meet me at the airport and I'll be escorted on the climb." I saw Mom flinch at the word *climb*, but DJ was on it. "Actually, it's not really a climb, more of a long hike. You just have to take it slowly because of the altitude. And Grandpa's supplied everything: airline tickets, guides, money, the works. It'll be a piece of cake. Really."

Mom looked slightly mollified, and I silently thanked DJ for being so relaxed and responsible. "What has he asked *you* to do?" she said, turning to look at me.

Taking my cue from DJ's performance, I launched in. "He's asked me to go to Barcelona to research what he did there in the thirties, when that picture I showed you was taken." DJ was nodding encouragingly. "He's paying for an airline ticket and a bank card and he's given me a contact address."

"I don't know." Mom looked worried.

I plunged on. "Barcelona's much closer, and more civilized, than Kenya, and I've got the name of someone at the address who will be my guide while

I'm there." That last bit was stretching the truth, but I didn't want Mom to worry.

"He does seem to have organized everything," she said uncertainly. "I'll need to think about all this and talk it over with Vicky, Deb and Charlotte."

"We'll be fine, Mom," DJ said. "We're responsible seventeen-year-olds, and Grandpa organized everything. We'll keep in touch and everything will be great. It'll be a wonderful adventure for us both, and it was Grandpa's final wish." DJ could play the emotional card as well as Mom.

"You're probably right," Mom said. "It's all just a bit sudden and overwhelming. I *do* want you boys to do what Dad wanted, I just need to get used to the idea. And there will be a lot of details to organize. We'll talk about all that later." I noticed a tear forming in the corner of her eye. "I love you boys."

"We love you too," DJ and I answered simultaneously.

"If it's okay," DJ said, "as soon as we get ourselves organized, we'll come to you for some help. Right, Steve?"

I nodded. "Sure." DJ was doing fine, and I was happy to let him run with it.

"We'll need to get stuff for our trips: clothes, backpacks, guidebooks, not to mention travel insurance. Stuff like that. Could you help us?"

It was a stroke of genius on DJ's part. Mom hated the idea that she might be left out of our lives as we grew up. Make her part of our lives, ask for help and give her a task to do, and she was as happy as anything.

"Okay." Mom became businesslike again. "That's a good idea, and I'd be happy to help you both get organized." She stood up. "But now I have to get the spaghetti on. I'll call you when it's ready."

I headed for my room. DJ followed me. "I think we're okay," he said as soon as the door closed.

"Yeah," I agreed. "You did an awesome job out there, calming Mom down and getting her to help. D'you really have a guide meeting you?"

"Yes. You don't?"

"I've got a name and an address," I said sheepishly. "Grandfather doesn't actually say it's a guide. You won't tell Mom, will you?"

DJ laughed. "Don't worry, I won't tell. What is it you have to do? My task is easy—climb a mountain. You were kind of vague out there."

"Grandfather was kind of vague," I said. It only took me a moment to decide to share the contents of the envelope with DJ. I owed him for easing the way with Mom, and if I was honest, I was proud of what I had worked out so far. I showed DJ everything and ran through my list of clues and conclusions.

"It's not much to go on," he said when I was done. I felt disappointed at his response, but before I could get annoyed, he went on, "But I suppose that's what a mystery's about."

"I guess so," I said, "but I wish I could find out more before I go."

DJ smiled slyly. "I think I might be able to help."

"How?"

"The slogan on the wall in the photograph."

"The Communist symbol?"

"Not that," DJ said, his grin broadening. "The other bit."

"Mac and pap? I ran them through Google and only got weird stuff."

"Did you run them through together?"

"No." I spun round to the keyboard and typed in *"mac pap."* The very first hit was a Wikipedia entry for the Mackenzie-Papineau Battalion, commonly known as the Mac-Paps. DJ sat patiently, his smile not fading, while I read the entry.

The Mac-Paps had been formed in Spain in 1937 by Canadians who had gone there to fight in the civil war. They were a part of the International Brigades, tens of thousands of Socialists and Communists from fifty-three different countries, who had gone to Spain to help the government fight the Fascist Army rebellion. They had fought bravely, but lost and left Spain in 1938.

"How did you know that?" I asked.

"I told you to take grade-eleven socials," DJ said with a laugh. "That field trip to Ottawa—one of the places we went was a memorial to the Mackenzie-Papineau Battalion on Green Island. Apparently almost sixteen hundred Canadians went to Spain and only half of them came back. Anyway, do you think that might explain what Grandpa was doing in Spain?"

"Maybe. The timing's right and a war would certainly have been dangerous enough." I wrote *Mac-Paps* on my list. After a moment's thought, I added a question mark. "Of course, the graffiti could simply have been a coincidence."

"You'll make a good scientist one day. You don't make assumptions about anything until you're certain. But didn't you notice what the Mac-Pap's motto was?"

I hurriedly scanned the Wikipedia entry again. "Of course," I said. "Their motto was, 'Fascism will be destroyed,' the slogan written on the back of the photograph."

DJ nodded and stood up. "Another piece of your mystery," he said. "Well, we've got a mountain *and* a mystery. I wonder what the others got." He moved to the door. "Good luck with the Spanish thing."

"Good luck with your mountain." Just as DJ was leaving, I added, "And thanks for your help."

He shoved his head back in and winked broadly at me. "No problem, little brother."

"You too, bro," I said to the closing door.

I was so happy I couldn't even get annoyed. DJ had been a big help, with both Mom and the Mac-Paps. I was making progress. Suddenly, the two pieces of poetry fit into the puzzle.

I understood that *they* in the first verse must be the volunteers of the International Brigades coming from all over the world to fight. They had clung to expresses, floated over oceans and walked passes to present their lives. But they had been beaten, that was the meaning of *History to the defeated / May say Alas but cannot help nor pardon.* The graffiti wasn't a coincidence. I scored out the question mark on my list.

So, my grandfather had gone to fight in a war in Spain in 1937 and 1938; that was dangerous and dramatic. He had been in Barcelona at an address I knew, and he might have been a Communist. I had discovered a lot, and I would learn more about the Mac-Paps, the Spanish Civil War and Communists. But there were still a host of questions that needed answering. Why had he gone? What had he done there? Why had he never spoken of it to anyone? Who was the girl in the photograph? What had Grandfather left at the address? There was still plenty of mystery to keep me interested.

FIVE

I squinted out the airplane window at the sun-touched peaks of the Pyrenees Mountains. Had Grandfather trudged all night up narrow valleys and over high passes, terrified that a dislodged rock would alert the border guards? Probably. As far as I could tell from the research I had done since the will reading, most of the foreign volunteers hiked into Spain to join the International Brigades. I was glad to be flying. I was on the last leg of my journey from Canada, an overnight charter flight from Manchester to Barcelona, full of loud tourists headed for the beaches and cheap rum of the Mediterranean coast.

If my guesses about my grandfather being in Spain in 1937 or '38 were right, then he was a fairly late arrival in the Spanish war. The fighting had begun in the summer of 1936 when the army had staged a Fascist revolt against the elected Republican government. The army's shot at grabbing power had failed because the workers in the cities, mainly Madrid and Barcelona, had armed themselves and fought back. The revolt had led to a civil war that had dragged on until 1939. What made the war international was that Hitler in Nazi Germany and Mussolini in Fascist Italy had immediately supported the Spanish army with thousands of soldiers, tanks, planes and weapons.

The thing that had shocked me when I was reading about the war was how little the democratic countries—Britain, France, the United States and Canada—had done to help the Spanish Republic. They had refused to sell arms or supplies to the Spanish government, even while the German and Italian Fascists were pouring help into the Spanish army. I had discovered that the Canadian Prime Minister, William Lyon Mackenzie King, had commented in his diary that he thought Hitler was "really one who truly loves his fellow man" and had "nice eyes"!

How wrong could someone be? The more I read, the angrier I became. I began to wonder if it was this kind of anger that had made Grandfather go and fight in Spain.

The plane banked to begin its descent into Barcelona airport, and I was treated to a beautiful view of the sun rising over the broad expanse of the Mediterranean Sea.

"Look at those beaches," the middle-aged woman beside me said, leaning over to peer out the window. As we had taken off from Manchester and before I had closed my eyes to feign sleep, she had told me that she was from Wigan in the north of England, looking for "a bit of fun." Her name was Elsie and she was on a package trip to the Costa Brava with three friends from work. "Two weeks of sun, sand, drink and parties." She smelled strongly of cheap perfume.

"You going to look for a young lady?" she said, winking and prodding me knowingly in the ribs as the plane swooped toward the runway.

"I'm going to find my grandfather," I replied.

She seemed disappointed. "Oh. He lives down there then?"

"He's dead," I said, "but I think he fought in a war here a long time ago."

Elsie gave me a long look. "Young fella like you shouldn't be bothering about boring old history. It's the present that matters, not the past." She turned to her friend in the seat next to her. "Hey, Edna, this young fella doesn't know how to have a holiday. What d'you say we take him with us and show him a good time?"

Edna was younger than Elsie, but beneath a thick layer of makeup, it was hard to tell by how much. "Come with us, son," Edna said with a terrifying leer. "I'll look after you."

I must have looked nervous, because Elsie laughed and said, "Don't worry, lad. I won't let Edna get her talons into you. But don't be so serious. Make sure you leave some time for fun."

"I will," I said as the wheels touched down at the end of the runway. I said it confidently, but I was more nervous than I had ever been in my life, arriving alone in a foreign city with only an address that I knew nothing about. What if the person at the address wasn't interested in helping me? What would I do for the next two weeks? If I thought about it rationally, I knew I would be fine. I had the bank card and some cash, a guidebook and a few basic phrases of Spanish. I would get by, but I felt horribly lonely. And my task made me nervous. I was good at solving problems, specific problems with a concrete answer I could work toward. The problem Grandfather had set me hadn't been clear. What was I supposed to find out? A part of me wished I was going on a mindless, no-stress holiday on the beach.

"Come on," Elsie said to Edna as she stood and rummaged in the overhead bin for her carry-on luggage. "We're wasting beach time." She looked back at me as the brightly dressed, cheerfully babbling tourists filed down the plane's aisle. "If you get bored with the history stuff, we're at the Hotel Miramar in Lloret de Mar. You find yourself a nice young lady and come and visit us. I hear the disco there plays lots of that hip-hop music you youngsters like."

"I'll try." I smiled back weakly and grabbed my carry-on bag.

By the time I had collected my backpack, lined up interminably to be examined by Spanish customs and immigration, and fought my way through the crowds of arriving tourists to the front of the terminal building, I was exhausted even though it was still not quite seven in the morning.

As far as I could see in either direction, the sidewalk was a seething mass of sweating people hauling huge suitcases that must have contained enough clothes for three months, jostling into vast snakelike lines for cabs that were arriving one or two at a time, or shouting at hotel buses that sailed past with full loads. The prospect of spending most of my morning here wasn't thrilling, and my guidebook said that if I walked out of the airport to the main road, there were buses that ran regularly to downtown Barcelona. I hoisted my backpack onto my shoulders and set off.

As soon as I left the airport and the crowds, I felt better. The surrounding countryside was flat, treeless and crisscrossed by highways and dotted with industrial buildings, but the roads were quiet and the air pleasantly warm even though the sun was only just up. It felt good to be on my own and in charge, even if I was only catching a bus.

At the bus stop, I flipped open my cell phone. I had a new text.

Hey Mom and Steve too. I hope you are doing well. All is good here. Just getting ready to meet and start out. I figure 2 days up and 1 down. Back on the plane soon after and back home in less than 5. Don't worry about me. Everything is perfect—see you soon...and little brother remember if you need help I'm only a text away.

Typical arrogant DJ, going to climb a mountain like it was the same as going to Safeway. And he'd probably do it too. Easy for him with guides and everything, and here I was alone in a foreign country with only the sketchiest idea of what I was to do.

I almost ignored the text, but then I sent back, Doing my task. If u need any help let ME know.

The first bus that came along said *Plaça de Catalunya* on the front. I knew that Catalunya was downtown and not too far from the Gothic Quarter where my address was, so this was perfect, except that the bus was crowded. It was a long bus, jointed in the middle, and every inch was packed with seated or standing men and women in jeans, T-shirts, jackets and caps. There wasn't a suit or tie in sight. They were obviously not office workers.

I stepped back, prepared to wait for the next bus, but the vehicle wheezed to a stop and the doors opened. I waited for people to get off to make room for me and my backpack, but nothing happened. I peered in the double doors halfway along the bus's length. A sea of tanned faces smiled down at me. I hesitated. There was no room. A chorus of unintelligible words broke out and hands waved me on. Uncertainly, I stood on the step. Immediately I was grabbed and hauled in among the tightly packed bodies. My backpack disappeared over everyone's heads to the back of the bus and the doors closed behind me. The bus jerked forward. I felt like a sardine and wondered nervously if I'd ever see my pack again.

The guy beside me, his face inches from mine, smiled and said, "*Benvingut. ?Com estàs?*"

They were words I hadn't learned. In fact, the way he said them, they didn't even sound Spanish. "*Hola,*" I tried. "*Buenos días. Mi nombre es Steve.*"

The man shook his head. Everything about him was dark: his hair, his eyes, the shadow of a beard on his chin, even his black leather jacket. "No," he said. "No *Espanyol.*" He dragged his right arm up from the crush and pointed to his forehead. "*Catalan.*"

He managed to wave his hand over his head to include everyone on the bus. "*Catalan*," he repeated.

I nodded. I had read that the people around Barcelona called themselves Catalan instead of Spanish, but I hadn't realized that they spoke a completely different language.

"Aina," the man shouted over his shoulder. A disturbance ran through the crowded bus and a young woman pushed her way forward. All I could see of her was her head with her hair tied in a tight bun at the back. The man said something long and incomprehensible to her. She looked at me and smiled, her white teeth standing out dramatically against her olive skin.

"You are English?" she asked.

"I'm Canadian," I replied.

She nodded as if that explained everything. "Welcome to Catalunya," she went on. "My name is Aina. You would say Anna in English. My friend, Agusti"—she nodded at the man who had tried to talk to me—"speaks only Catalan." She lowered her voice, "Actually, he speaks Spanish, but he does not like to." The man gave Aina a withering look.

"You speak English very well," I said.

Aina smiled once more. "Thank you. I worked in London for two years as a barmaid. Now Agusti and I work at the factory making boxes for the gears in cars."

"Transmissions," I suggested.

"Yes," Aina said. "What is your name?"

"Steve." Aina looked puzzled. "Steven," I expanded.

"Ah, Steven. In Catalan, it is Esteve, in Spanish, Esteban. You have come here on holiday for our sunshine and beaches?"

Before I could answer, the bus pulled into another stop. A number of workers got off and headed into a large factory complex. This reduced the crush, but the group around me stayed where it was as Aina said something in Catalan. I assumed she was telling them about our conversation, because everyone looked at me and smiled. As we started up again, Aina looked at me expectantly.

"I haven't come for the beaches," I said, thinking back to my companions on the plane. "I have come to find out what happened to my grandfather many years ago."

"Your grandfather was in Barcelona?"

"Yes, in 1937 or '38. I think he might have been a soldier in the war."

Aina suddenly became very excited and rattled off a whole string of Catalan, the only piece of which I understood was "*Brigadas Internacionales.*" Suddenly everyone started talking at once and jostling to pat me on the back as if I was some kind of hero. I was happy and embarrassed at the same time.

When the activity calmed down, Aina explained, "The foreigners who came to fight for Spain and Catalunya in our war are heroes here."

A male voice somewhere behind Aina burst into song and was joined by others.

Viva la Quince Brigada,
rumba la rumba la rumba la.
Viva la Quince Brigada,
rumba la rumba la rumba la
que se ha cubierto de gloria,
¡Ay Carmela! ¡Ay Carmela!
que se ha cubierto de gloria,
¡Ay Carmela! ¡Ay Carmela!

Aina leaned forward and shouted in my ear. "It is the song of the Fifteenth Brigade who are covered in glory. Your grandfather was in the Fifteenth Brigade?"

"I don't know," I shouted back. Most of the bus was singing now. "I suppose that's one thing I'll have to find out."

Aina looked out the bus window. "We are almost at our work now." She rummaged for a piece of paper in the bag hanging from her shoulder. She wrote for a moment and then handed it to me. "This is the name and address of Pablo Aranda, the grandfather of my cousin. He is an old man but still alive, and he lives in a village by the River Ebro, we call it the Ebre. As a boy in the war, he was rescued by some soldiers. Perhaps if you go to his village, he might tell you stories."

Aina hesitated and looked at me with a frown. "He is a strange old man. He will not be what you expect, or wish. But he is part of history as well, and if you want to discover what happened, you must discover it all, not just what you would like to believe."

I looked at the torn piece of paper. *Pablo Aranda, Avinguda Catalunya, 21, 43784 Corbera d'Ebre.* "Thank you," I said. I was about to ask what Aina meant by the old man being strange, but I was cut off by her smile. The singing had died away, and the bus was slowing down.

"Stay on to the Plaça Catalunya," Aina said. "It is the center of Barcelona. You can go anywhere from there. Good luck."

As the workers poured off the bus, most smiled at me, shook my hand and wished me what I assumed was good luck. As the bus pulled away, Aina stood on the sidewalk and waved at me. I felt stupidly happy. If all Spaniards—Catalans, I corrected myself—were this friendly, I was going to enjoy my task. And I had another address. I seemed to be collecting them.

SIX

"Plaça Catalunya," the bus driver announced. There were only half a dozen of us left on the bus, me and five office workers in suits who had boarded a few blocks back. I hauled my backpack from the luggage racks at the back of the bus, said "*Gracias*" to the driver and got off. It was only as I stood on the sidewalk, watching the bus pull away, that I realized I hadn't paid for the trip. The driver had said nothing, so I assumed Aina or someone else had taken care of my fare. Another example of Catalan generosity.

It felt as if I had already met guides, but there was only one who really mattered. I looked around the square to get my bearings. According to my map, the Ramblas, the street that led down to my address, was diagonally opposite. I set off.

Even this early in the morning, the Ramblas was awesome. It was really two streets with a wide pedestrian precinct with trees down the middle. Although it was only eight in the morning, a few outdoor cafés already had tables out, and scattered customers sat sipping coffee and reading newspapers. Casual strollers wandered past with no apparent objective other than to glance in shop windows. The shops were still closed and shuttered, and it made me think that I was maybe too early to go to the address Grandfather had given me. The last thing I wanted to do was wake up Marie Dolores Calderon Garcia, whoever she was.

I strolled down until I came to Carrer de la Portaferrissa. It was exactly as it had looked on Google—a narrow alley, about 4 meters wide and surrounded by ancient four- or five-story buildings. At this time in the morning, the street was in deep shadow and the few pedestrians just darker shapes in the distance. I knew that number 71 was at the far end, but the Ramblas seemed a much better place to kill time, so I turned back, selected a café and sat.

My guidebook recommended coffee and a pastry for breakfast. In fact, it said it was all I was likely to get outside an expensive hotel, so, using a few learned phrases, I stumbled through an order. The waiter seemed to think it was very funny, but eventually brought a tiny cup of brutally strong coffee and the sweetest pastry I had ever tasted.

I sipped the coffee but wolfed down the pastry since it was all I had eaten since getting on the plane the night before. I ordered another and a glass of water and took out my cell phone. I felt a bit bad about the way I'd blown off DJ's text at the bus stop. His arrogance annoyed me and he was always so formal. I don't think he liked texting, he preferred to talk or send an email. He claimed that texting was butchering the English language. Of course that just made me use as many chat abbreviations as I could, just to mess with him.

Dwntwn Barca, I texted, hvng a cb, u cld pave 403 w/ this stuff. evry1 really friendly, but they speak odd. gl w/ mountain. u'll b on top by lunch tbl bro.

Then I texted Mom. It was the middle of the night in Toronto, but I had promised to let her know I had arrived safely. I sent it in plain English. Everything is great. People really friendly. On my way to the address to meet up with my guide. "I hope," I murmured under my breath as I folded my phone.

People came and went, the traffic became heavier and eventually the shutters on some of the shops rolled up. I paid and set off down Carrer de la Portaferrissa. I was nervous as I passed through the shadows below the narrow wrought-iron balconies. I had come all this way chasing a mystery. The address had been my goal through all the preparations. Now I was only a few doors from it. What if no one was there? What if the mysterious package was just something meaningless, or not even my grandfather's? Worst of all, what if they knew nothing about a letter or a package or me?

I would be fine, I told myself. I had a ticket home and money to live on, but I would have failed. The other six, even Rennie, the mystery grandson, probably all had specific tasks like DJ's mountain climb. They would all complete their tasks, I was certain. I would be the lone failure. As I had researched the Spanish Civil War, I had begun to see Grandfather differently, not as the old man I knew, but as the kid with the weird haircut in the photograph. He had walked this very street when he was my age. Why? What was he doing coming here in the middle of a war? Would I find out? Would I—?

And then there I was, standing in front of the doorway in the photograph. It looked older, more worn. My eyes drifted to the wall beside it, as if I expected to see the faded hammer and sickle and the words *Mac Pap*. There was nothing.

Well, this was it, the moment that would determine the next two weeks. Whether I succeeded or failed. I stepped forward and raised my fist to knock. Before I had a chance, the door flew open and the girl from the photograph stood there, smiling exactly as she had all those years ago. The insane thought that she was a vampire, one of the ageless undead, flashed into my mind before I squashed it. That was stupid, even for me.

It wasn't the same girl. Not only was that impossible, but now that I looked closely, this girl was different. There was a similarity around the mouth and she had dark hair and an olive complexion, but I was starting to understand that was pretty common in Spain. The nose was the clincher;

it wasn't at all like the one on the girl in the photo-graph. Hers had been small and straight. This girl's nose was longer and narrower, more like mine, and it was slightly skewed, giving the impression that her head was continually tilted slightly to one side as if she was questioning everything.

All this flashed through my mind in the first second I stood staring, slack-jawed at her, but it was her eyes that made my knees go weak. They were the deepest brown I had ever seen, so deep that I almost felt I was falling into them.

"Are you going to hit me?" the girl asked in perfect English.

Horrified, I realized I was standing in front of this beautiful girl with my fist raised threateningly. I snapped my arm back to my side. "No. Of course not. I was about to knock. I'm sorry," I babbled.

The girl's smile broadened. "You are lucky, Steve. I was just on my way out. I expected you earlier."

"Sorry," I blurted out again before I realized what she had said. "How do you know my name?"

"Your grandfather told me."

"My grandfather told you?" The more I said, the stupider I sounded. But how *could* my grandfather have told her? She wasn't the girl in the photograph and, as far as I knew, my grandfather had never been to Spain after the war. "How?"

"In the letter he wrote to me."

"The letter?" My brain seemed to have stopped working.

"Yes," the girl said patiently. "My great-grandmother wrote your grandfather a letter and he wrote back. Then I heard from your grandfather's lawyer that you would be arriving on an early flight this morning and would be coming here. That's why I expected you before now. A taxi from the airport does not take this long."

"There weren't many taxis," I said, "so I took a bus, and had a coffee."

The girl nodded as if what I had said made any sense. "Well, now that you have had your coffee and are here, shall we go inside?"

"Yes," I mumbled and followed her through the door.

It took my eyes a moment to adjust to the gloom inside, but I could soon make out a row of mailboxes along one wall on my right. The girl was already climbing stone stairs ahead of me.

On the first landing, the girl produced a key and opened a second heavy wooden door and waved me into a wide corridor. Doors opened off to the left and right, but we proceeded down the corridor's full length into a wide room, brightly lit by floor-to-ceiling windows that overlooked the street. The high ceiling was carved dark wood, and the walls were almost completely covered with framed pictures, both old black-and-white photographs and paintings. What wall space was left was covered with overloaded bookshelves, and a variety of old-fashioned chairs were scattered around a low wooden table. The floor, too, was wood but was covered in the center by a worn red patterned rug.

"Welcome to my home," the girl said. "Put your pack down; it looks heavy."

"It's okay," I replied, although I was glad to set it on the floor.

"My name's Laia," the girl held out her hand. "Welcome to Barcelona."

I shook her hand. "Thank you. I'm Steve, but you know that."

"I do, and I have some things for you, but sit down." Laia indicated a high-backed chair. "I will fetch them and get us a cup of coffee. If you haven't had too much already."

"Coffee would be nice," I replied, "but not too strong."

"You do not like our *café solo*. Don't worry, I make regular American coffee."

Laia left the room, and I had a chance to gather my scattered thoughts. My concerns about no one at the address knowing anything about my task had proved groundless. The opposite seemed to be the case, and my mind was full of questions: What had my grandfather said in his letter? Who was this girl, Laia? And what connection did she have to what I was supposed to do?

All these questions raced around my brain, but I didn't really mind not knowing. Laia's eyes dominated my thoughts. I smiled. I doubted DJ was meeting beautiful girls on his mountain.

"You look happy," Laia said. She was carrying a tray with a tall silver coffee flask, a smaller jug of milk, a sugar bowl and two cups.

"Just glad to be here," I said.

Laia placed the tray on the table in front of me. "Please pour yourself a cup as you like it. I like mine black." As I busied myself with the coffee, she went to an ornately carved sideboard, knelt and pulled out a small battered suitcase.

The suitcase was a faded checked pattern in black and brown. Where it was scuffed, it appeared to be made of cardboard, although the corners were reinforced with leather strips. It was considerably smaller than an airline carry-on bag and sported a number of old-fashioned stickers, including one for something called Trans-Canada Air Lines and another for Canadian National Steamships. It was closed by two locking silver clasps on the front.

Laia set the suitcase on the table beside the coffee cups and sat down beside me. We both stared at the suitcase for a long time. Was the answer to my mystery inside? What did the suitcase and its contents mean to Laia?

"Have you looked inside?" I asked eventually.

"I cannot," Laia replied. "It is locked and there is no key."

I almost laughed out loud. "Yes, there is," I said, pulling my keychain from my pocket. The old key looked the right shape to fit the suitcase's locks. I reached forward and then stopped. I was excited and nervous at the same time. I doubted the suitcase contained a simple answer, so what would I find inside? More mysteries?

Laia noticed my hesitation. "Perhaps you should read this first," she said, producing a new white envelope she had been holding by her side. "It came with the letter from the lawyer. It is addressed to you."

I put the keys down, took the envelope and tore the flap open.

Hello again, Steve,

If you are reading this, it means you have taken me up on my challenge and are in Barcelona. I hope you have met Maria and that she has agreed to help you and has introduced you to the collection of memories in my old suitcase. That is where you should begin.

I find myself envying you and the discoveries you are about to make, but some of the things you will find out will be hard. I know they were almost impossible for me to live through. That is a life lesson I learned in Spain: the most wonderful passion can exist alongside the most brutal pain. But I must allow you to find things out in your own way.

I can visualize every scrap of paper in that suitcase, and there have been countless hours over the past decades that I have sat and imagined going through it as you are about to do. That suitcase contains a piece of my life. A piece that no one except Maria knows about and that does not even exist in my mind, now that I am gone. Yet, if, at the end of my long and eventful life, I were offered the chance to relive any three months of my life, despite the pain, it would be my time in 1938 in Spain.

I have traveled all over the world, but I never voluntarily returned to Spain. After I was shot down in the Second World War, I was smuggled through Spain on my escape, but that was all very secretive and I barely knew where I was. After the war I was not allowed back into Spain—had I gone anyway, I could have been thrown in prison or worse. Later, when it would have been safe for me to return, I didn't because I convinced myself that there was nothing left there for me. The letter I received from Maria proved that I was horribly mistaken in that assumption, and I sometimes wonder how my life could have turned out differently. Of course, I have had the best life a man could hope for, filled with the wonderful love of my wife, my children and my grandchildren. Still, I can't help but wonder.

I think, if I am honest with myself, it was fear that stopped me ever going back. Not physical fear, although I experienced enough of that in Spain to last a lifetime.

Oddly, I think it was two opposite fears: fear that Spain would not be as I remembered it, and fear that it would be too much as I remembered it.

To you, this is probably just an old man becoming nostalgic. I hope it will mean more in time. What is important now is your present and your future, and I fervently hope that the suitcase before you will give you a tiny fragment of the wonder and passion that was mine so many years ago.

Good luck with your quest.

Give my love to Maria, and know that I love you and wish you everything you wish for yourself for a long and happy future.

Grandfather

SEVEN

I let the letter drop and stared at the battered suitcase. This was it, what Grandfather had wanted me to find. There was a tremendously important part of his life in this case, a part that no one else knew about and that I was about to discover. I felt as if he was sitting beside me, more alive than he had ever been when I knew him. But something was wrong.

I looked up at Laia. She was watching me intently. "Where's Maria?" I asked. "Who is she?"

Laia lowered her gaze to the table and blinked rapidly. When she looked up at me, there were tears in her eyes. "Maria was my great-grandmother," she said softly. "She died the night before this letter arrived."

"I...I'm sorry," I stammered. I felt helpless. More than anything, I wanted to put my arm around Laia's shoulder and comfort her, but I'd only met her minutes ago. "You were close?"

Laia took a deep breath and wiped her eyes. "Yes, we were very close. She always claimed that I was her soul mate and that watching me was like once more being young. She said looking at me was like looking in a mirror that turned back time." Laia smiled sadly. "We both have a very stubborn streak. Even when she turned ninety years old and the stairs took her an age to climb, Maria refused to leave this place. She said that it had always been her home and that her past was here. She told me many times that without a past we are nothing more than fallen leaves that blow around the park at the whim of any breeze that comes along. Our past anchors us and makes us real. That is why you are here, no? To discover your past."

"My grandfather's past," I said.

"It's the same," Laia said with a shrug. "The past does not begin when you are born. It is a line, a thread that winds back through your parents, grandparents and all your ancestors. You live in Canada?"

I nodded.

"Then at some time an ancestor of yours stepped onto a boat in the Old World to seek a better or a freer life in the New World. He or she is a part of you, just as the Moors who ruled this country a thousand years ago are a part of me."

Laia sipped her coffee. "But listen to me go on. We have just met and already I am lecturing you as if we were in a class at the university. It is a failing of mine. I have no brothers or sisters and no interest in the dancing and parties that my school friends find so entertaining, so I spend my time with books. They are very good companions, but not so good at conversation."

"It's okay," I said hurriedly. In truth, under normal circumstances, I would happily have sat all day listening to this girl talk endlessly about anything she wished, but my eyes drifted to the suitcase.

Laia noticed my glance. "But the past you seek is much more recent."

I pulled the suitcase closer and reached forward with the key. Laia placed her hand on top of mine, halting the movement. "I don't know what you will find in here. I know it is very important to you, but I also know it was very important to my great-grandmother. One night, as a child, I came through to get a glass of milk and found Maria sitting at this table, just as we are now, staring at the suitcase. In all the years of keeping it, she never opened it, but I suspect that there is a piece of her past, and mine, in here as well."

"Then we'll discover it together," I said.

Laia squeezed my hand and then released me. With the skin of my hand still tingling from her touch, I fitted the key into the lock and turned it. There was a soft *click*, and the silver latch sprang up. I repeated the process on the other side and, with a quick look at Laia, lifted the lid.

I don't know what I expected to find. With all the mystery, Laia's talk of the importance of the past, and the weird jet-lagged feeling that I was somewhere else on a different day, nothing would have surprised me. What we found ourselves staring at was a collection of yellowed newspaper cuttings, a crumpled, dirty red scarf, a brown dog-eared pamphlet entitled *Spain in Arms 1937*, a shapeless piece of black metal about the length of my thumb and a khaki beret with a red enamel star pinned to it.

I picked out the lump of metal and turned it over in my hand. It was heavy and obviously part of something much larger, but there was nothing written on it to say what that might have been. I looked at Laia, and she shrugged. I placed the metal to one side and reached for the beret. It was filthy and tattered and didn't look much like something someone would come halfway around the world to find. It felt as if it would crumble to dust in my hand. "Was this my grandfather's?"

"Maybe. It is very old, and the red star was the symbol of the Communists in the war."

Laia reached in and pulled out the red scarf. "I think this was Maria's." The scarf was simply a large, square handkerchief. It was frayed along the edges and one corner was torn off. Laia lifted it to her nose. She closed her eyes and spoke softly. "Maria was sixteen when the war broke out in 1936. There was much fighting in the streets of Barcelona in those first days, between the army and the people. Some fighting was nearby on the Ramblas, and Maria once showed me where the streets were barricaded.

It is still possible to see chips in the old bricks where bullets struck."

Laia lowered the scarf and stared at it. "Maria took messages between the different barricades. No one had any uniforms in those days, so she was given a red scarf to wear round her neck to show that she was one of the people and not a Fascist."

A sudden thought struck me. I put the beret down and reached for the travel pouch that hung around my neck under my shirt. As Laia looked on with a puzzled expression, I pulled out my passport and took the old photograph from inside the back cover. "You look very like her," I said, passing the picture over.

Laia gasped. "That's her. I've only ever seen pictures of her when she was older. Everything was lost from that time." She reached out and gently touched the surface of the photograph as if she could make contact with the smiling young woman standing in the doorway. Her finger slid over to the young man. "Is that your grandfather?"

"Yes."

"When was the photograph taken?"

"In 1937 or '38, I think."

Laia nodded. "Maria would have been seventeen or eighteen. Look," she said, pointing at the young Maria's neck. "Do you think that could be this scarf?"

"It's hard to tell from a black-and-white photograph, but it's possible."

Laia stared for a long moment at the photograph. "He looks like a nice young man, your grandfather," she said eventually. "They look so happy."

"They do," I agreed. "And Maria was very beautiful."

"But we must get on," Laia said, handing me back the photograph.

We almost bumped heads reaching forward to retrieve the next item from the case. I pulled back, flustered. Laia laughed lightly and lifted the pamphlet out. The cover was dark orange and made of cheap creased cardboard. It showed a charcoal sketch of a determined-looking man holding a rifle and running forward. The title, *Spain in Arms 1937*, was at the top and the author's name, *Anna Louise Strong*, at the bottom, along with the price, *25c*. Laia examined it and passed it over to me.

The pamphlet was more a small book, over eighty pages long, and it smelled musty. I thumbed through it, looking at the chapter headings: *Heroic*

Madrid, Front Trenches, The International Brigades.
Someone—Grandfather?—had underlined sections in blue pen. Most had no comment, but one caught my eye. Underlined was, *I would rather die stopping fascism in Spain than wait until it comes to Britain.* In the margin beside it, someone had scrawled *or Canada!*

As I reached the back of the small book, a folded page fell out. It was so cracked along the fold and stained and worn that large pieces were unreadable, but it seemed to be a small poster advertising a meeting in Toronto in 1937. The headline was *Stop the Bloody Hands of Fascism in Spain,* and it had been distributed by the Communist Party of Canada.

While I was looking at the book, Laia had been gently lifting out the first few newspaper cuttings. Some were in English and some in Spanish. One was the front page of the *New York Times* for July 18, 1936, with the headline, *Spain Checks Army Rising in Morocco.*

Laia pointed to a clipping from a Spanish paper called *El Diluvio.* Most of the page was taken up with huge black letters that screamed *NO PASARAN!* "That was the slogan from the defense of Madrid in the first months of the war," she explained. "It means *They Shall Not Pass*."

Silently and carefully we lifted the last of the cuttings out. All were about Spain and all were dated 1936 through 1938. Underneath them was a colored poster, the same size as the bottom of the suitcase. It showed old-fashioned biplanes with garish red stars painted on the sides, flying in formation over a muscular arm ending in a clenched fist.

It was all very interesting, but I was disappointed. The beret and the scarf were links to the young couple in the photograph, but they couldn't tell us a story. The book and the newspapers *could* tell a story, but it was one I had mostly discovered on my computer at home. How did all this help my quest? Laia reached in and lifted out the poster. She began to translate the Spanish slogan below the raised fist, but I wasn't listening. The poster wasn't the last thing in the suitcase.

The book at the bottom of the suitcase was thin and not much bigger than my passport. It was covered in plain brown leather, worn at the corners and heavily stained. One particularly large stain spread darkly out from one corner over almost a third of the cover. As I reached for the book, Laia looked up from the poster. "What is it?"

The leather cover was stiff with age. I opened it to the first page. The paper was very thin and, unlike the newspapers, hadn't yellowed. The page was covered with closely spaced lines of writing that made me draw in a sharp breath. The writing was neater, but there was no mistaking my grandfather's hand.

JUNE 15, 1938

Here I am at last, standing on the Spanish earth. My dream is coming true! All the months I have spent reading about the struggles of the Spanish people against the rich, self-interested landowners, the blood-soaked hands of the Church and Franco's brutal war machine have led here. What better time to begin a journal?

At last I can do something. Even if my government is happy to sit complacently and watch or, even worse, help Franco, Hitler and Mussolini crush all freedom under the iron heel of Fascism, I am not. I will fight and, if necessary, die beside my comrades from Canada and all around the world, to see the Spanish people freed from tyranny and Fascism stopped in its tracks.

NO PASARAN!!!!!!

This won't do. I have just read back what I have written. Why is it that the thoughts I truly and passionately believe in seem so stilted and preachy in black and white on the page? I want to tell everything of the adventure I am beginning, but I will do it in two ways. I shall collect newspaper cuttings and anything else that will tell the broader picture, and I shall reserve these pages for my personal story. There will be no more lecturing from me.

I doubt I shall be able to write every day. Some days will probably be too busy, and in any case, this is a small volume in which to record everything. I shall, however, jot down thoughts and significant events as they occur and as I find time.

First, where am I? I am sitting in the dust beside a rough road in the foothills of the Pyrenees, waiting for a truck to take us to Barcelona. From there we will join our units in the International Brigades for training. I shall join the Mackenzie-Papineau Battalion of the XVth Brigade.

Dawn is brightening the clouds to the east, but the air is still chill. My comrades and I have spent the night climbing and scrambling over mountain passes from

France, terrified that every dislodged rock will alert a border guard who will turn us back, or worse, open fire. But we made it.

We are eight in number, myself and another Canadian called Bob, three Americans from New York, an Englishman, a Frenchman and a German escaping Hitler's regime. We are all exhausted by the night's journey, and all except me are trying to catch a few minutes' sleep. I can't; it's all too exciting.

An old man—a peasant with ragged clothes, wooden clogs and an unbelievably weather-beaten face—has just walked past along the road. As he drew level, he turned, raised a clenched fist and greeted us with "Salud." Only our guide, Pedro, and I were awake enough to respond.

I can hear the rumbling of our truck in the distance, and Pedro is waking my colleagues. I shall continue this when I have a chance.

EIGHT

Laia coughed softly, dragging me back to the present. "It's Grandfather's journal," I said. "He began it the morning after he and some others walked over the Pyrenees. He was on his way to join the other Canadians who were fighting in the Fifteenth International Brigade."

I let my hand slide gently over the words on the page. "He wrote me and my cousins letters before he died. He wrote the way he talked, and reading them was like he was still alive. This is different. He sounds so young and enthusiastic, but old somehow too. I guess that's how people wrote back then."

"It is a voice from a different time," Laia said. "He *was* young, just like Maria, but he must have had much enthusiasm—and courage—to bring him all the way here from Canada." Laia shook her head in wonder. "They were the same age as us and they were in a war. Perhaps young people grew up more quickly in those days."

"I guess they had to," I said. "And I thought coming here on my own to look for Grandfather's things was a big adventure."

"Is this what he wished you to find?"

"I think so."

"Good, but I do not think you should read the whole journal right now. I know some things that might help you understand better, and I have an idea." Laia glanced up at a large clock across from us. "But we have been here a long time. Do you like pizza?"

"Yes," I said, surprised by the sudden change in topic.

"Good," Laia said. "I know a place on the Ramblas that will interest you." She stood up. "Shall we go?"

"Sure," I replied, standing. I looked at the clock. It was after eleven and I had eaten only the pastry since yesterday. "Pizza sounds awesome."

Laia smiled. "On the way, I shall show you some history."

*

"You speak very good English," I said as we walked along narrow streets between ancient buildings that seemed to be reaching above us to block out the narrow strip of blue sky.

"Thank you. Maria spoke a little English— perhaps she learned from your grandfather—and she taught me when I was small. My mother insisted I take English in school. She said it was the language of the computer, the Internet, and that speaking it would open up more opportunities for me. I spent a summer in England and an English boy spent a summer with us, so I had plenty of practice. And I love languages. I speak Spanish, Catalan, English, some French, even a little bit of Latin, but I don't get to use that much."

I felt completely overwhelmed—and impressed. The few Spanish words and phrases I had learned for this trip had been a struggle. I couldn't imagine learning three languages. Something Laia had said gave me the chance to change the topic. "Where are your mom and dad? You don't live alone, do you?"

"No, I don't," Laia said with a grin. "I live with my mother, but she is away just now helping my grandmother. Grandfather has"—Laia's brow furrowed as she searched for the right word— "a confusion of the brain."

"Alzheimer's," I volunteered.

"Yes, that's what it's called. He cannot live at home anymore, so he must go into a home. My mother and my grandmother are moving him this week. I was going to help, but I stayed because you were coming."

"Thank you," I said, feeling ridiculously happy that she had. "Is your dad helping as well?"

"My parents separated when I was five years old."

"I'm sorry," I said, feeling stupid.

"No need," Laia said. "Mother says that she married my father too young. They were not well matched and it took some years, and my arrival, I think, for them to see that. He lives in Sevilla. I visit him sometimes, and he sends me presents at Christmas and on my birthday."

The street we were on abruptly opened out into a small treed square with an ornamental fountain in the center. It was empty apart from a group of small boys kicking around a soccer ball in front of an ornate doorway. The walls on either side of the doorway were heavily chipped and pitted. Even with the noise of the boys, the square exuded a sense of peace and quiet after the bustle of the narrow streets we had been walking along.

"This is cool," I said.

"It's your first history lesson," Laia explained, walking over and sitting on the rim of the fountain. Water ran over the lip of a raised stone bowl and splashed into a green-and-white-tiled basin. "This is *Plaça de Sant Felip Neri*. It is very old."

"And peaceful, even with the kids playing."

"Yes, it is," Laia agreed. She pointed to the door behind the boys. "That is the church of Sant Felip Neri. It was built in the eighteenth century. During the war, the Fascists bombed Barcelona, and the church was used as a refuge. One day, a bomb landed here and killed twenty children who were sheltering."

I looked at the boys kicking the ball about and wondered what the bombing had been like. "Is that why the walls are so pitted?"

"No, the bomb fell through the roof and exploded inside. The scars on the walls are from the end of the war. After Barcelona fell to the Fascists, people were brought to this square, lined up over there and shot. See, all the marks are at chest or head height."

I sat in silence, staring at the bullet holes in the wall and trying to imagine the last moments of the terrified people who had stood in front of it. "Why are you telling me this?" I asked eventually.

"There is a lot of history in Barcelona, and in Spain. Some would say the problem is that we have too much history. History has soaked into everything here—the earth, the walls, the people, even those children playing over there. It's a violent and sometimes tragic history, and your grandfather was a part of it.

"I don't know what's in that book from the suitcase," she continued, "but I know from Maria that it is from a very brutal and tragic time. I brought you here to show you that because I want you to be certain before we begin that you are prepared to go wherever the book might lead you."

"I am," I said, although I wasn't certain. I had assumed that the quest Grandfather had sent me on was a mystery adventure. I would find out things from the clues I had been given and it would all be fun. Laia seemed to be presenting a much darker side to what I was undertaking. I suppose I should have taken what she said more seriously, but I couldn't stop one word racing excitedly around my brain. Laia had said she was telling me this before "we" began. The prospect of spending the next two weeks in the company of this incredible girl swamped any worries she was trying to create.

"Okay," Laia said. "Then I will tell you the idea that I had. Maria once told me that she had known a young man who had fought in the Fifteenth International Brigade. She said she had nursed him after he had been wounded in the battle along the Riu Ebre in 1938."

"The Ebre?" I interrupted.

"Yes, that's what we call the Ebro River. You know it?"

"Not really. Someone mentioned it to me once," I explained, thinking of Aina on the bus from the airport but not wanting to stop Laia's flow. "Go on."

"Maria never gave me any details about the soldier or even told me his name, but the look in her eyes when she mentioned him was so sad and faraway that I knew he must have been important to her."

"My grandfather?"

"I think it must have been. Maria told me this last year and a few days later asked me to go on the Internet and see if I could find an address for an organization of Canadian Spanish Civil War veterans. I found one. I think she used it, and that's what triggered the response from your grandfather." Laia fell silent and stared into the sparkling water of the fountain. At last she looked up. "I wish she had sent a letter earlier. Maybe they could have met."

"That would have been awesome," I said, but I didn't really mean it. If Maria and my grandfather had met, then I wouldn't be here now, and there was no way I wanted to change that.

"Anyway," Laia said, "after Maria told me about the brigader, I spent a long time wondering who he might have been. I found out as much as I could about the war, the Fifteenth Brigade and the battle of the Ebre River. This summer I was going to visit where the battle happened; it's not too far from the city. When I heard that you were coming,

I decided to wait. Perhaps we could tour the battlefields together?"

"Yeah!" I almost shouted. Mentally I slapped myself for being such an idiot and tried to say something intelligent. "If Grandfather mentions places in his journal, we could visit them."

"We could," Laia said, her face wreathed in a smile. "You have the journal, and I shall be your tour guide. When I heard you were coming, I did some research and printed out information from a website about the battle. It lists the memorials for the Ebre battle with pictures and maps. We shall use them. They are in Spanish, but I shall translate for you."

"You can be my guide," I said, thinking that whoever was helping DJ up his mountain could be nothing like my guide through the history of this strange and complex land. "And we can read the journal as we go, as close to where it was written as possible."

"That's a good idea. We can start tomorrow on the train to the Ebre. It's only a few hours' journey."

"Yes," I said, afraid to say more in case I started babbling inanely. All the talk of death and tragedy vanished, replaced by the thought of traveling with Laia.

"Then that's what we will do," Laia said, standing. "But I have kept you waiting for pizza long enough. On the way, more history. I will show you my street."

"Your street?" But Laia was already on her way out of the square. I jumped to my feet and hurried after her.

Laia led the way for about 30 meters down yet another narrow street and then abruptly turned right. I almost bumped into her as I turned the corner.

"*Baixada de Santa Eulalia*," she said. "The Descent of Saint Eulalia. She is the patron saint of Barcelona, and her body lies in the cathedral. Perhaps I will show you if we have time."

"What happened to her?" I asked, still confused as to why this was Laia's street.

"About three hundred years after Christ, Eulalia was asked by the Romans to deny Him. She refused and was tortured thirteen times, once for every year of her age, ending with decapitation. It is said a dove flew out of her severed neck. Legend has it that it was on this street that she suffered one of her tortures, being rolled along inside a barrel with knives sticking through it. So, the Descent of Saint Eulalia."

"Another cheerful Barcelona story," I said. "But why is it your street?"

"That is my name," Laia said with a mischievous wink. "Laia is a short form of Eulalia. I am named for a saint, just like you, except your Saint Stephen was only stoned to death." With a laugh, Laia set off again.

JUNE 29

The planes come over in broad daylight, so low I feel I could reach out and touch them. They are black and evil and fly in a V formation like the geese in the fall back home. It is possible to see the bombs fall, small objects that wobble stupidly on the way down. They look harmless until the explosion rips through a building, tearing down walls, shattering windows and shredding clothing and flesh.

If there is time, people run for shelter in the subway, but often the planes appear with no warning. The bombers have complete freedom of the sky, although this morning a solitary squat biplane, a Chato I was told, appeared and attacked. One of the bombers peeled off and limped away, smoke trailing from one engine, but the Chato burst into flames and crashed into the sea.

What good is the pilot's bravery with the odds so heavily stacked in the enemy's favor? And it is Canada's fault! If we, and the United States, Britain and France, supported the Spanish government, there would not be one obsolete Russian fighter but a squadron of modern fighters able to sweep the black German and Italian bombers from the sky.

Oh dear, I am preaching again, but it is hard not to. There are political slogans everywhere, on posters on ruined walls, on the crackling radios that people huddle around for news, in the speeches that we new recruits must listen to every day. It is a time for slogans.

Since the truck brought us down from the mountains, my life has been a chaos of new sensations and experiences. Barcelona is a wonderful city, but it is being steadily ground to dust by the bombers who come every day and every night. The Spanish people I have met are wonderful, coping with the bombs, food shortages, no running water and only occasional electricity with a cheerfulness I couldn't imagine if this were Toronto. Of course they believe passionately in what they are fighting for, and that makes a huge difference.

We new recruits have been installed in a large ornate building on a street called Ramblas. In a few days we will be taken to our units in the countryside, but first we must be indoctrinated with the correct political ideas. Twice a day we sit and listen to a huge bear of a man with a strong

Russian accent—Bob has nicknamed him Winnie the Pooh—explain why we are fighting and how it is a step toward the worlwide workers' revolution, after which we will all live in a paradise similar to the one in Russia.

Bob scoffs at the whole thing. "We know why we are going to fight," he says. "We volunteered. We disobeyed our own governments and traveled halfway round the world to risk our lives. I don't think we need Winnie to tell us."

Of course he only says this quietly to me. On the first day of lectures, one of the Americans—his name's Carl and he's a Communist taxi driver from the Bronx—asked if a rumor he had heard that the International Brigades were to be withdrawn from Spain was true. Winnie flew into a towering rage, yelling and screaming for almost an hour about how that sort of rumor-mongering only helped the Fascists and how anyone who helped the Fascists would be taken out and shot. No one has asked a question since then.

The Englishman is odd. He insists that his name is Christopher, although the Americans persist in calling him Chris. I think they do it to annoy him. Christopher is tall and blond and speaks as if he has plums stuck in his cheeks. He comes from a very *wealthy family and has a First Class Honors Degree in Classics and Romance Literature from Cambridge University. He is also an ardent Communist and hangs on Winnie's every word.*

The Americans, whom Christopher calls Yanks, tease him mercilessly, but he takes it all in good spirits. Their favorite topic is how America had to come to bail England out in the Great War. Christopher simply smiles, thanks them and observes that at least they have showed up for this war on time.

We are a mixed bunch and shouldn't really be together. Each nationality—American, British, French and German—has their own battalion, but it is not as clear as that. There are so few volunteers now and there were so many casualties in the spring retreats, that it is much more mixed. In fact, I've heard that most of the battalions of the International Brigades are made up of Spanish conscripts. Anyway, we are to be kept together. There was some talk of putting us with the Americans in the Lincoln-Washington Battalion, but the decision has been made for us to join the Canadians. I'm pleased.

When we are not listening to Winnie, we are taken out to help clear up bomb damage. It's hard physical work, but what's worse is seeing people's lives reduced to smashed furniture, ripped clothes and torn photographs. Yesterday I found a porcelain doll in the ruins of an apartment. It was beautiful and expensive. What happened to the little girl who treasured this doll?

There is a hospital in the basement of our building run by an American nurse with Spanish help. It's for soldiers and was busy after the fighting south of here in March and April. At the moment, it's mostly filled with injured civilians from the bombing. I got talking to one of the Spanish nurses who wanted to practice her English. She said how grateful everyone was that foreigners like me were coming to help the Spanish people. It made me feel very proud. She lives close by and has invited me round for lunch tomorrow. I'm looking forward to it.

Much as I like Barcelona, I wish we were going to join the Mac-Paps (the nickname for the Canadian Battalion) and get on with our training. We came here to fight, after all.

NINE

As the train noisily hauled itself out of one more deserted station and continued its rumbling journey through Aragon's dusty hills, I passed Grandfather's journal over to Laia. She had asked if she could read it, and I saw no reason why not. My only condition was that I got to read a section first and that she would not read on past where I had got to.

I watched Laia across from me, engrossed in the journal. I could barely sit still for the three-hour journey from Barcelona's train station, Estació de França, to Flix on the Ebro River. My doubts about what I was undertaking and my concerns about traveling on my own had vanished. Here I was, unraveling my grandfather's mystery with a beautiful Spanish girl to help me. Perhaps she could become more than simply my guide. DJ was welcome to his mountain.

Laia glanced up and caught the stupid grin on my face as I stared at her. My ears burned with embarrassment, and I hurriedly turned to stare out the window at the endless regimented rows of gnarled olive trees marching across the parched, red hillsides.

After her history lesson yesterday, Laia had taken me to a place on the Ramblas called Café Moka for one of the best pizzas I had ever tasted. However, I was wrong in thinking the history lesson was over. "There was fighting here in 1937," she had said, "between the Communists and the Anarchists."

"Why?" I asked. "Weren't they on the same side?"

"Yes, but it was not as simple as one side or the other. The Communists hated the Anarchists because they would not obey orders without discussing them first. The Communists thought that the Republic had to be centralized and organized to win the war. The Anarchists thought people should make their own decisions, even in war. The English writer George Orwell was here then and got caught up in it all."

"The guy who wrote *Animal Farm*?" I asked.

Laia nodded. "He had been wounded and lived across the street from where we are now. When the fighting broke out, he fought against some Communists in this café."

I looked around at the shiny, clean counters and modern art on the walls.

"It was very different then," Laia had said.

I was learning that there was history everywhere and that Laia seemed to know most of it.

"Maria told me about the bombing of Barcelona when she was a girl," Laia said, pulling me back from my memories of our pizza lunch yesterday. She closed the journal and looked out the window on the far side of the carriage. "There it is," she said.

I followed her gaze. We were traveling beside a wide brown river flowing sluggishly between high banks. "The Ebro?" I asked.

"Yes," she said. "It won't be long until we arrive at Flix."

"Did Grandfather fight here?"

"I don't think so, although part of the battle was fought here." She looked back at me. "Perhaps you need to know the background to the battle your grandfather fought in."

"How come you know so much history?" I asked.

Laia thought for a minute. "I suppose because we have so much in Europe and a lot of it is violent and has happened in our backyards. But don't distract me. Your lecture's about to begin."

I laughed. If all my teachers were like Laia, I would have taken every socials and history class that was offered.

"By the time your grandfather crossed the mountains, the war was going badly. The Fascists had reached the sea south of here and split the Republic in two. The bombing of Barcelona was intense, the border with France was closed and the port was blockaded by Franco's navy. The Republic was running out of everything and it was only a matter of time before the Fascists marched down the Ramblas."

It struck me as strange that Grandfather had chosen this time, when the war was so nearly lost, to come and fight. Maybe the journal would tell me why.

"The only hope was that a war against Fascism would break out in Europe. Then Britain and France would surely have to help Spain."

"But Grandfather was here in 1938 and the Second World War didn't start until 1939," I said, proud to show off what little I had learned about history.

"Yes, but it almost began at Munich the year before."

I couldn't compete with Laia. "What happened at Munich?"

"The Munich Agreement?" Laia looked at me. I stared back blankly. "The crisis over Czechoslovakia?"

I shook my head.

"In 1938, Hitler threatened to invade the borderlands of Czechoslovakia. If the democracies tried to stop him, there would be war."

"So the Second World War could have begun then?"

"Easily."

"Why didn't it?"

"For the same reason the democracies didn't support the Spanish government against the Fascists: they were scared. The British and French prime ministers had a meeting with Hitler in Munich and agreed to give him the bits of Czechoslovakia that he demanded."

"That's harsh," I blurted out.

"Yes," Laia agreed. "For his part, Hitler promised that he wouldn't invade anywhere else. The next year his army went into the rest of Czechoslovakia, and even the most frightened politician realized that war couldn't be avoided.

"The idea here was that one big victory would encourage Britain and France to help Spain. The Republic got together everything they had left, including the surviving International Brigades, and planned a surprise attack over the Ebro River. That's what your grandfather was part of."

"At Flix?"

"All along the river here, but the Fifteenth Brigade crossed near Flix. I think it's a good place to begin. Now read some more of the journal." Laia handed Grandfather's book back to me. "Perhaps it will tell us where to go after that."

JUNE 30

We have our orders! Tomorrow we will be taken out to join the Mac-Paps in the countryside where they are training. A new month and a new adventure.

Bob and I shall not miss Winnie one bit, but I shall miss Barcelona. In the past two weeks, despite the dangers of the constant bombing, I have grown to love this place. The people are unfailingly friendly and will go out of their way to help. Two days ago, I mustered almost all the Spanish I knew and asked an old man for directions to a hospital, where I was to collect some blood serum for our wounded. Not only did he point the way, but he insisted on taking me the entire distance, even though it was far and well out of his way. For the entire journey, although I understood little of what he said, he insisted on telling me stories and pointing out buildings of note. When we reached the hospital, to my great embarrassment, he embraced me and shouted "Viva las Brigadas Internacionales!" before setting off back the way we had come. These are people worth fighting for and, if anything Winnie says is to be believed, tens of thousands of them are being shot out of hand by the Fascists.

I went for lunch today with the nurse who lives nearby. Her family welcomed me as one of their own and freely shared what little food they had. Unfortunately, they had considerable wine, and after a couple of glasses on a near-empty stomach, I committed the unpardonable sin of dozing off during Winnie's lecture this afternoon. As a punishment, I was made to clean the toilets out back, a truly disgusting job that I had avoided up until now.

Despite scrubbing my skin raw, I still smell like a barnyard and barely have the strength to hold this pen steady. I wanted to put down the good news, but now I shall sleep and dream of a tomorrow without Winnie.

JULY 1

Dominion Day for the Canadians. No Red Ensigns or patriotic songs, but the Mac-Paps' flag was held high and the Internationale sung lustily. The flag is a large rectangle of red bearing the words CANADA'S MACKENZIE-PAPINEAU BATTALION, 1837–1937, FASCISM SHALL BE DESTROYED. It also sports a raised fist over a red star and a green maple leaf. It's very grand, and I got a lump in my throat as we sang beneath it.

We new recruits have been formed into a squad under a Canadian officer. His name is Pat Forest, but everyone calls him Tiny because he is over six feet tall and almost that wide across the shoulders. He's a dedicated Communist and was a stevedore on the Vancouver docks. He's been over here since January 1937 and has been wounded FOUR times. The men say it's because he's such a large target.

As I had been told, most of the Mac-Paps now are young Spaniards. Some of them look even younger than I do! Tiny told us that there are Canadians scattered in other units as well. He knows of several boys in the Dabrowski Battalion because they had recently immigrated to Canada from Eastern Europe and they felt more comfortable with the language in that battalion. It's all very strange, but there's a feeling that nationality doesn't matter. We're all here for the same reason.

The Mac-Paps suffered heavily in the spring battles, but despite that, the mood is good and everyone is certain that we will win the battle that all know is coming soon.

"We'll beat those sons-of-guns," Tiny declared this afternoon. Actually "sons-of-guns" is not what he really said, but I don't feel comfortable writing down the real word. "The governments in Canada, Britain and America will see what we can do and finally realize that we have to stand up to Fascism, and the sooner we do it, the better it'll be. They don't even need to fight, just give us some decent tanks, planes and machine guns, and we'll do the job for them. If we win in Spain, you just watch Hitler and Mussolini run scared. Like all bullies, they're cowards at heart."

"And as we march triumphantly into Burgos to put Franco on trial for war crimes, we'll look up and see a flock of pigs winging their way overhead." This was from Hugh, a short, skinny guy who peers out from behind thick round spectacles; he's the only veteran apart from Tiny in our squad. He was a schoolteacher in Winnipeg before he was fired for corrupting the young minds of his students with Communist ideas. He's just back from having a bomb fragment dug out of his thigh and still has a limp. Hugh's the wet blanket in the squad, always there with a negative point of view whenever anyone says anything positive. What he said annoyed me, but the others simply shrugged it off with a laugh.

"Have you all forgotten what it was like back in March and April?" Hugh went on. "We had nothing to stop those German panzer tanks, bullets just bounced off them, and where was our air force? All I ever saw were a few relics that were blasted out of the sky as soon as they showed up. Those damned German and Italian bombers owned the sky, and the worst were those dive-bombers, coming straight down at us with those sirens wailing." Hugh fell silent and absent-mindedly rubbed his wounded leg.

"Listen to him," Tiny said to us with a broad grin. "He thinks the dive-bombers were specifically after him."

"Might as well be," Hugh said bitterly, limping off. He threw a final comment over his shoulder. "They'll get us all sooner or later."

"Pay him no mind," Tiny told us. "This time we've got tanks. They came over when the French border was open this summer. If no one messes up, we'll have surprise on our side too. Franco's concentrating on taking Valencia to the south, and he's getting hung up on the defensive lines there. Our attack'll come as a shock. Now, let's get you lot started on some training, else all the surprise in the world won't do us a bit of good."

Tonight Bob and I have bedded down with the rest of the squad in a ruined stone farmhouse. There's no roof, but that doesn't matter. I don't think it ever rains here, and it's nice to look up and see the stars. I'm writing this by the light from the stub of a candle stuck on a tin plate. Bob's asleep and I will be soon. I just wanted to put down a few thoughts first.

Life here is hard and we haven't even started to fight yet, but I'm happy. Everything's much simpler *here than at home and, if I'm honest, which I promised I would be in these pages, that's one of the main reasons why I left. Oh, I came to fight against the Fascists, and now that I'm here I'm fighting for the wonderful people I've met and to stop those black bombers flying over Barcelona, but I was running away as well. Running away from boredom and not knowing what I'm going to do with my life.*

Well, enough of this maudlin dwelling on the past. I must get some rest. I will write more when I get the chance.

TEN

The bright sunlight stabbed my eyes as the train rushed out of the tunnel. I squinted and the Ebro came into focus, meandering around a narrow neck of land. Perched on the highest point of the peninsula stood the rounded walls of a ruined castle. Modern buildings spilled down the hillside almost to the water's edge, and trucks bustled over a long bridge in front of us. The train slowed as it approached an open platform.

"Is this Flix?" I asked.

"Yes. This is where we start," Laia said. She closed the journal after her turn to read and passed it over to me.

Then she stood and retrieved her backpack from the overhead rack.

I got my backpack down and stuffed the journal safely into one of the outside pockets. "We still don't know where we go from here. The last sections of Grandfather's journal weren't much help."

"No," Laia admitted, "but he's not writing every day and he doesn't fill the pages with a lot of trivia. I don't think it will be long before we get to the battle. It started on July twenty-fifth. Let's find a hostel and then walk up to the castle. That will give us good views in both directions along the river. If we read enough of his journal, that should tell us where to go tomorrow."

"Okay," I agreed as the train lurched to a stop. I was enjoying Laia being my guide and taking care of everything.

✦

We found a small guesthouse only a few blocks from the station. The owner, a tiny, stooped, ancient woman dressed entirely in black, looked at us suspiciously when Laia asked if she had any rooms.

She cheered up when we explained that we required separate rooms.

The rooms were small but cheap. My feet hung off the end of the bed and we shared an equally cramped bathroom down the hall. We had a brief argument over who should pay. I felt that I should use Grandfather's money for everything on this trip. Laia insisted that she pay her share, so we compromised—I would pay for the rooms and she would buy our food.

As we left to climb to the castle, the landlady engaged us in conversation. She had obviously been waiting by the front door to tackle us at the first opportunity, and undoubtedly news of our visit would be all over town by the time we returned from our walk.

Laia told her that I was Canadian and that my grandfather had fought here during the war and we were here to research what had happened to him.

For half an hour, we were treated to a monologue about how hard life had been when she was a girl. Laia translated the main points as best she could. Apparently there had been little actual fighting in Flix itself, although the town had been bombed because the Republican headquarters had been in the railway tunnel we had passed through and there had been several pontoon bridges on the river nearby. As important to her was the fact that sugar had been impossible to buy and the bread was disgusting and very expensive.

As we tried to edge out the door, the woman turned to me. She grabbed my arm with a surprisingly strong grip and stared in my face. I was surprised to see a tear in the corner of her eye. "*Gracias*," she said.

I mumbled, "You're welcome," without really knowing what I was being thanked for.

"*Gracias. Gracias*," the woman repeated. Tears were now streaming freely down her wrinkled cheeks. To my utter embarrassment, the old woman let go of my arm, raised her clenched fist in the air and, in a voice quavering with age and emotion, launched into the song that I had first heard sung on the bus from the airport. "*Viva la Quince Brigada, rumba la rumba la rumba la...*"

I stood uncomfortably as she sang to me. When she was finished, she wiped her eyes on her sleeve, hugged me and scuttled back inside the house.

"Wow!" I said as we went off through the narrow streets. "What was that all about?"

"She was thanking you for the International Brigades," Laia replied.

"But the war was over more than seventy years ago. I had nothing to do with it."

"True, but as I told you, you carry your past with you. Your grandfather fought here with the International Brigades. She cannot thank him, so she thanks you. We are Spanish; we carry a very heavy past, and the war years and the hard times after it are still remembered by those who lived through them. Even today we are still finding mass graves and learning about the many thousands of babies that were stolen at birth and given to nuns for adoption by Fascist families. The past is very real for us."

We walked the rest of the way up the hill to the castle in silence. I was deep in thought. Were the old woman's tears part of the passion that Grandfather had talked about? Had the war meant as much to him as it obviously did to her? If so, why had he never talked about it? I was finding things out, but I was no closer to discovering the things that Grandfather seemed to want me to understand on this journey.

The rough stones of Flix Castle were warm in the afternoon sun. Laia was right; the views were spectacular in both directions. I tried to imagine two armies fighting and dying on the banks of the river, but it all seemed too tranquil—the farmers working their fields, seagulls swooping above the water and the occasional small fishing boat drifting with the sluggish current.

"I'm going to wander around the ruins," Laia said. "Why don't you read some more and see if your grandfather tells us where to go next."

"Okay," I said. Laia wandered off, and I settled myself as comfortably as possible against a smooth section of wall and opened the journal.

JULY 15

Two weeks since I added to these pages. If I'm going to keep my promise to write down what is happening I have to force myself to write despite the tiredness.

We are still in the ruined farmhouse, although there are rumors that we will be moving soon. Every day we train for twelve or fourteen hours. Some days we go to a nearby river and practice launching small boats and rowing them over, but mostly we simply charge over rough hills and practice digging ditches and building low walls to hide behind. There is some weapons practice, but since there is only one rifle for every two men, this is only occasional. Most excitingly, there has been some training in advancing with tanks. We don't have actual tanks—they are being kept in a safe place until the attack—so we have to imagine that officers carrying huge red flags are mechanized vehicles.

Tiny is wonderful—generous with his time for us new recruits but stern when he has to be. Bob was goofing off during an exercise the other day, and Tiny tore a strip off him in front of everyone. "This is not a joke," he said. "War is not a game. The things I am trying to teach you could save your life in a few days. More importantly, they could save the life of the man beside you, and we need every man alive and fighting if we are to win this battle."

Bob, and the rest of us, were suitably chastised and have taken the work more seriously since then.

Hugh continues with his negative comments. Just this evening, we were talking about the tanks that are to support us. "A whole bunch of officers carrying red flags will certainly scare the Fascists," Hugh observed.

"That's just for training," I said. "The real tanks will be here when we need them."

Hugh turned his gaze on me. "How are we going to get across the Ebro?"

"In the boats we've been practicing in," I said, confused by his apparently stupid question.

"How many men does each boat hold?" he asked.

"Eight. You know that."

Hugh nodded. "And how many tanks?"

"What do you mean?" I said, annoyed at my own confusion. "That's a dumb question. The boats are far too small to carry tanks."

Hugh smiled and continued as if he was explaining something to a five-year-old child. "The Fascists are on one side of the river and we're on the other. Assuming—and it's a big assumption—that we manage to keep this attack secret and they don't manage to shoot us all to hell in the river, we get across and establish a bridgehead. Say we're lucky and we push forward for a couple of days. What do we do then?"

"We keep going," I said.

"Supported by our wonderful tanks?"

"Of course."

"As you so cleverly pointed out, a tank won't fit in one of our boats, and I doubt very much if the

Fascists have been kind enough to leave us an intact bridge over the river."

"We've got engineers," I said. "They'll be following up to build bridges."

"And the Fascist dive-bombers will be overhead cheering them on. You're a good kid, but you've a lot to learn. The only victories we've ever won have been defensive. The Fascists have better planes, better artillery, better tanks, better rifles and more of everything. Every time we go into the open, we get cut to pieces. It's happened over and over again and it'll happen this time too, sooner or later."

Hugh wrapped himself in his blanket and turned away from me. His negativity annoys me intensely, but part of me wonders if he might be right! I'm tired. I must get some sleep now before I dwell too much on this.

JULY 18

We were at rifle drill today when the bolt blew out of one of the older rifles we have. It tore a huge gash in the cheek of the man holding it, Horst, the German refugee who crossed the Pyrenees with Bob and me. I think it broke his cheekbone as well. He was extremely lucky not to lose an eye. He was evacuated to Barcelona, sitting in the back of an ambulance, his face covered in bloody bandages and his fist raised in defiant salute.

Hugh was standing beside me and commented on how lucky the man was to be missing the upcoming battle. I'm afraid I lost my temper. "If you don't want to fight," I said, "why don't you just leave? You're nothing but a coward."

Hugh glared at me, and for a minute I thought he was about to hit me, but then he burst out laughing. "All sensible men are cowards," he said, "but I'm not going anywhere. I came here to fight and to kill Fascists, and I've been doing that for the past year and a half. I'm not about to stop now. There's hardly any of the original boys left. Me and Tiny're about all there is from the twenty-five who trekked over the mountains on Christmas Eve 1936. If this war goes on much longer, I wouldn't put money on me seeing another Christmas. If that's what happens, so be it. I made a commitment to something and I'm not about to back down, but I'll be damned if I'll go cheerfully to my death, blind to all the stupidity and mistakes that have cost far too many good men their lives. Everyone lies, kid," Hugh said, patting me on the shoulder. "Learn that, and maybe you'll live a little longer."

What a strange man Hugh is.

I wonder if Horst will be tended to by the nurse I met in Barcelona.

JULY 20

I have a hat. A beret actually. There is very little regulation-issue headgear, so everyone wears whatever they have or can scrounge. Had I known this, I would have picked something up in Barcelona.

Anyway, I have been talking to Marcel the Frenchman we traveled with. Despite all the evidence to the contrary, he assumes that because Bob and I are from Canada, we can speak fluent French. In reality, I think he simply wants to practice his English because he has a bunch of distant relatives in New Brunswick and wants to go there one day.

Marcel owns a beret that he claims was once the property of the writer Ernest Hemingway when he lived in Paris. I doubt that is true, although the beret looks old and worn enough, and Marcel does say that he is planning on writing a book about his experiences in Spain. He puts me to shame by writing voluminous notes in a large red notebook at every opportunity.

This morning, Marcel acquired a wide-brimmed canvas hat from a local farmer in exchange for a bottle of cheap brandy he had brought from Barcelona. The hat is in no better condition than the beret, but the brim helps keep the blistering sun off. I had admired Marcel's beret, and since I didn't have a hat of any sort, he offered it to me. It is only a loan and Marcel insisted that I promise to return it after the battle.

I pinned my badge on it and wore it proudly all day. Bob says I look like a Parisian gangster and Hugh commented that a steel helmet would be more use, but I am happy.

JULY 21

Just a quick scrawl to say we have our orders. We move out tonight for the Ebro. It's not long now. I'm so excited I can barely hold this pen still. This is what I came for. I wish I'd written more before. I don't know when I'll get another chance to write.

JULY 22

In a barn, somewhere. We march at night and hide from the Fascist planes during the day. Thankfully, there are few planes about, otherwise they could not *fail to notice that something is afoot. Men stream along every road and track, and trucks rumble back and forth incessantly. It's tiring, but all our spirits are high. I haven't seen any tanks yet, but then, I suppose they are being kept hidden until the attack.*

JULY 23

Still in the barn. It's boring and hot. When will we move forward?

Christopher sang us a song this evening. Apparently it was written by a Brit at a place outside Madrid called Jarama. It's sung to the tune of "Red River Valley," but the words disturbed me. They are not about glory and what we are fighting for but about a bunch of bored soldiers thinking they have been forgotten. I persuaded Christopher to tell me the words.

There's a valley in Spain called Jarama,
That's a place that we all know so well.
For 'tis there that we wasted our manhood,
And most of our old age as well.

From this valley they tell us we're leaving
But don't hasten to bid us adieu

For e'en though we make our departure
We'll be back in an hour or two.

Oh, we're proud of the British Battalion
And the marathon record it's made
Please do us this one little favor
And take this last word to Brigade:

"You will never be happy with strangers,
They would not understand you as we,
So remember the Jarama Valley
And the old men who wait patiently."

"It's not about the war or fighting," I pointed out.

"My young friend," Christopher said in his upper-class voice, "soldier's songs rarely are. If you are in the business of killing and dying, you don't want to sing about it. Only those not in war make up songs like that. Soldiers sing about home, sweethearts and boredom."

"It just doesn't seem very patriotic," I insisted.

Christopher smiled at me. "How about this then? At Jarama, the British Battalion of six hundred men fought for three days over a place they called

'Suicide Hill.' Four hundred of them didn't make it.
Is that patriotic enough for you?"

JULY 24

It is eight o'clock and the sun has just sunk below
the lip of the gully we are sheltering in. I will write
what I can before the twilight fades. We are not allowed
candles. In five hours we attack. The Mac-Paps are
in the second wave and will cross the Ebro tomorrow
morning. The Catalans will go ahead of us and clear
the far bank of the Moorish troops dug in there. We
cross between Flix and Ascó and head south to Corbera
and Gandesa. Tiny says it is about 12 miles to Gandesa.
Units south of us will be closer, but we will have an
easier time as we will follow a major valley most of
the way. Other units will have to fight over a series
of ridges. I hope he is right.

Tiny called us together this afternoon to let us know
about the attack. He took us to the top of a nearby
ridge, no easy task in the heat of the day. From the top,
we could see the castle of Flix to the north and Ascó to
the south. Neither are more than 1 or 2 miles away,
but they are in another world. The world across the
river, where we must go tomorrow.

Hugh asked what the orders were. Tiny smiled and said that they were simple enough even for Hugh to understand: "Go as fast and as far as possible toward Gandesa." I expected Hugh to retort with some comment about how were we supposed to win with orders like that, but he kept silent.

No one will sleep tonight. Those of us lucky enough to have rifles clean them obsessively. There is only one rifle for every two men, and Bob got one because he scored better than me on the range. He has promised to shoot the first Moor we see and give me his rifle.

This is it, what we all came for. Everyone sits silent with their own thoughts. No one jokes or fools about. Even Hugh has stopped complaining. Many of the men write letters on scraps of paper. I gave Bob a page from this journal and he wrote a letter to his parents. I have it in my pocket in case anything happens to him. This journal will be my letter. I have asked Bob to give it to the Spanish nurse in Barcelona.

Why did I do that? I barely know her. I suppose it's because this is such a different world, no one at home could understand. I'm not the same person I was only a few weeks ago when I crossed the mountains.

In some ways I've grown up. I guess, if I survive the next few days, I'll grow up even more.

Tomorrow, each of us will carry a pack that must weigh at least 50 pounds. Until the bridges are built, we will have to survive on whatever we can carry with us, scrounge from the locals or steal from the enemy. In addition to my blanket, mess kit and so on, I have several extra clips of ammunition (which will be no use if I have an enemy rifle with a different caliber); a sack of biscuits; a couple of small loaves of bread; three rings of red, spicy, dry chorizo sausage; several oranges; and, oddly, a tin of English corned beef. We all received one of the last items, so I suppose a shipload must have got through the blockade. I wish it had been loaded with rifles.

Water will be a problem, so I have my canteen and two extra leather pouches called botas. They take a bit of practice to use as they are held away from the mouth and the water, or wine, is sprayed in. It was messy to begin with, but I am getting the hang of it.

There is no moon tonight, so it is getting too dark to write much more. I will carry the journal in my tunic pocket and scrawl a few words whenever I get a chance. On to Gandesa!

ELEVEN

Laia and I stood on the highest bit of wall we could scramble up. We could just make out the roofs of Ascó, 5 kilometers south. Somewhere on the winding river between here and there, my grandfather, Bob, Tiny, Christopher, Marcel, Hugh, Carl and the other two Americans had crossed to go into battle. The temptation to read on was almost overwhelming, but I had resisted.

"Now we know where to go next," Laia said.

"Down to Ascó and then along the valley to Corbera and Gandesa."

"Exactly. We shall follow in your grandfather's footsteps."

"Are there buses?" I asked.

"Yes, but I have a better idea."

"What?"

Laia's face broke into a mischievous smile. "You'll find out tomorrow." She jumped down off the wall and headed back toward town. "Come on," she shouted back at me, "I'll buy you a plate of snails."

"Did you say snails?"

"You'll love them," she said with a laugh. "They're a local delicacy."

As I trotted after Laia, I thought of something else Grandfather had mentioned in his journal. "Do you think the nurse in Barcelona that he keeps thinking about was Maria?"

Laia stopped and turned to me. "I was wondering that too. Do you think so?"

"It's possible. I hope he mentions a name soon."

"Something else I was wondering," Laia said. "The beret must be the one in the suitcase." I nodded. "But your grandfather says that it was special to Marcel and it was only on loan. I wonder why he never gave it back." We walked the rest of the way down the hill in silence.

✦

As it turned out, we didn't get our snails right away. Our landlady was waiting for us by the guesthouse door. Without giving us a chance to say anything, she grabbed my arm and led us off down the street, babbling something over her shoulder.

"What's she saying?" I asked Laia, who seemed to find my predicament vastly amusing.

"She told you to come with her."

"As if I had any choice," I said.

"There is something she wishes to show you. Something from her childhood."

I groaned. What was there about her childhood that could possibly interest me? I silently prayed that whatever it was, it didn't involve hugging and bursting into song.

The old woman hurried us along about three blocks and stopped in front of a black wrought-iron gate. Above the gate was the silhouette of a plane with bombs falling from it. On one side was the word *Refugi* and on the other *Antiaeri*. A narrow passage led to a heavy black door in the hillside.

"Is this an air-raid shelter?" I guessed.

"Yes," Laia replied, and then we were through the gate and at the door.

A man almost as old as our guide appeared from a small room, and he and the old woman spoke rapidly. I caught the woman saying something about *Brigadas Internacionales,* and the old man stared hard at me. When she had finished, he stepped forward and grasped my hand. "*Gracias por su abuelo,*" he said as he pumped it up and down.

"He's thanking you for your grandfather," Laia said.

"*De nada,*" I replied, hoping that I'd got the expression for "Don't mention it" correct.

Obviously feeling that I was her exclusive property and that I had spent enough time with the old man, our landlady hustled me forward. The man produced a huge key, and as he unlocked the door and hauled it open, I was left to marvel at how everyone here seemed intent on thanking me profusely for something I had nothing to do with.

When the door was open, the man pulled a switch beside a large black box on the wall and lights flickered on all along a brick-lined tunnel. The roof was rounded and the tunnel seemed to end in a room carved out of the natural rock. The woman hustled me along.

The room, and other rough corridors leading off it, were lined with modern information boards showing maps, pictures of planes, different types of bombs and ruined buildings. There were also old pictures of the tunnels lined with people—men, women and children—sitting against the walls and staring at the camera with worried expressions. I wanted to look more closely at the pictures and have Laia translate the text for me, but the old woman was talking again and Laia was struggling to keep up.

"She spent many days and nights here when she was a girl," Laia said. "During the war there was a lot of bombing. You could feel the ground shake and stones fell from the roof." As Laia was explaining all this, the old woman jumped up and down and waved her arms in the air to simulate the ground moving and things falling down. "It felt like everything was going to collapse on top of you, and if you survived, you didn't know if you would have a house to go back to. You could hear the bombs fall above."

The woman was leaping around now, screaming, "*Boom! Boom! Boom!*"

Obviously unimpressed by my stunned reaction, she dragged me aside to one of the information boards and dramatically pressed a black button. A TV screen sputtered to life with images of black planes, bombs falling and exploding, burning buildings, walls collapsing and bodies, looking like limp dolls, scattered through the rubble in the streets. On the soundtrack, sirens wailed and explosions roared. As suddenly as it had begun, the audiovisual display ended, leaving us standing in overwhelmed silence.

"*La guerra,*" the woman said quietly.

"The war," Laia translated, unnecessarily. Even I knew that much.

As if returning to life, the woman plucked at my sleeve and led me to another board. This one was mostly taken up with a picture of people in the tunnel. She peered at the picture and pointed an arthritic finger at a little girl huddled in the middle distance. She wasn't clearly in focus but looked to be about five or six. She peered nervously out from between two adults, presumably her parents.

"*Esa soy yo*," the woman said.

I didn't need Laia to translate. "That's you?" I asked.

The woman nodded vigorously. "*Tenia cinco años.*"

"You were five years old." The woman grinned broadly to reveal a row of yellowed teeth. She grabbed my hand. I thought I was off on another excursion to her past, but she did the same to Laia. Spouting a long string of Spanish, the old woman forced us to hold hands and shoved us down the corridor toward the daylight. As we emerged, blinking at the brightness, I asked Laia what the woman had said.

Laia gave my hand a squeeze that sent shivers down my spine. "She said the war is over. Go and be young."

❖

The next morning, I texted DJ. hru bro? up the mntn yet? ig stories 2 tell. hagl. Then I suffered through our landlady's tearful farewell and promised to come back one day. I followed Laia to find out what method of transport she had in mind. We stopped outside a well-lit storefront. Lined up on the sidewalk outside were several brightly colored scooters.

"Scooters?" I said.

"Yes," Laia said proudly. "They are cheap to rent, and on them we can go wherever we want, not just where the bus goes."

"But I don't have a full license," I said. "I can't rent one."

"Yes, you can," Laia said, smiling. "If we get small scooters, fifty cc, we only have to be sixteen years old and we do not need licenses. We will not be able to win a race with a Porsche, but we have time."

Half an hour later, we were puttering through the narrow streets on bright blue scooters. I was a bit wobbly to begin with because of the weight of my backpack, but our machines were really easy to drive—they had electric starters and automatic transmissions—and they were cheap, only about $150 for four days. We made a brief stop to buy some sausage and bread before I followed Laia out of town into the hilly, dry countryside. As the sun rose higher and I watched Laia's dark hair fly out from under her helmet, I reflected that I had never felt happier. "Thanks, Grandfather," I murmured.

✥

After we turned inland at Ascó, the road was hillier than I had expected and dry. The only things that seemed to grow here were olive trees and grape vines, and they were pretty boring to look at after the first few thousand. I entertained myself wondering if Grandfather had walked over this or that hill.

After 15 kilometers, I ached all over and was getting tired of almost being sucked out into the middle of the road every time a huge truck roared past inches away from me. I was relieved when Laia turned off past a collection of stone buildings, and we came to a stop in front of some sort of memorial.

"This is the Memorial of the Camposines," she explained. "It is dedicated to the soldiers of both sides in the battle."

I slid off my scooter and gratefully dropped my backpack to the ground. Laia did the same but much more gracefully. She took a printed sheet from her pack and looked at it. "This is a memorial in two parts. That part," she said, indicating a concrete wall lined with colored information boards, "tells the story of ten soldiers who fought around here. They symbolize all who fought here. The other part"—Laia pointed to a set of steps disappearing round the corner— "is not open to the public. It is an"—she frowned in concentration—"an *ossario*, a place where the bones of the dead are kept."

"A graveyard," I suggested.

"Yes," Laia agreed hesitantly. "Bones are still being found in the hills around, so they are brought here for burial. Soldiers from both sides lie together."

I took a step toward the information boards, but Laia stopped me. "I have a suggestion. I will read the boards while you read the next pages of the journal. Then you can look around while I read."

"Sure," I said. I was happy enough to sit and get on with the journal, but I felt a bit like I was being ordered about. I was getting used to the country and feeling more comfortable traveling. I appreciated everything Laia had done and was doing—I would never have found out half as much without her—but a part of me wanted to have more say in what we did.

I'd escaped one big brother; I didn't want a big sister. Still, now probably wasn't the time to say anything about it. I retrieved Grandfather's book from my pack and sat on one of the wooden benches looking out over the wide valley.

JULY 25, SUNSET

How do I start? What can I say? How do I describe this day?

We are halted in an olive grove on a hillside south of Ascó. To write this, I am fighting exhaustion, the fading light and a strange weakness that comes from the release of tension. I have been elated, terrified, shocked and confused many times today, and my memories are little more than a series of images and feelings that I am not even certain come back to me in the right order, but I will try to tell what happened as best I can.

We went down to the river before dawn. There was firing from the other side, but the Catalans who crossed overnight had achieved complete surprise and pushed well over the first hills. We crossed eight or nine at a time in small boats that followed ropes strung over the river. Shells exploded up and down the river, sending tall columns of water into the dawn sky, but they were fired from far away and did no damage that I saw. The only casualty near me on the crossing was a young Spanish soldier who stumbled getting out of the boat, fell and broke his wrist. He was immediately ferried back across. Would Hugh say he was lucky?

There was a wonderful feeling standing on the far bank, a place that had been enemy territory until a few hours before. Men milled about, collecting equipment, piling supplies and organizing themselves into units for the advance. Engineers were already beginning to construct a rough pontoon bridge over the river.

Tiny kept us together and moved us away from the chaos of the river. We found a pile of captured rifles, German Mausers, and those without one helped themselves. Not much ammunition, but at least I now have a weapon. Passed a column of Moorish prisoners. They were being herded none too gently by some Spanish soldiers and looked sullen and downcast. They were an exotic sight in their red fez's and turbans, and wearing blankets over their uniforms.

As we stumbled up the first ridge, we suffered our first casualties. A random shell exploded to my left, almost deafening me but killing two men and wounding several, including one man who had his arm torn completely off. I saw it spiral through the air and land 10 feet from him.

I can't believe I wrote that so casually. Back home, something like that would be a major disaster, and I would have been horrified and sickened. Here someone simply applied a tourniquet, and the man and the other wounded were led or carried down to the boats. Have I become a monster, or is it the tension of battle? Oddly, the explosion and the man and his arm seem much more vivid and real now, many hours after, than they did at the time. Then it seemed at times almost as if I was simply an observer. Someone who has paid their nickel to watch a moving picture show.

Anyway, Tiny checked that everybody was all right (I found a piece of shrapnel wedged in my backpack), and we continued. We trudged over a couple of low hills, seeing quite a lot of abandoned Fascist equipment and more lines of prisoners. Shells still exploded here and there, but we were well spread out and I don't think they did much damage. We could hear firing in the distance and see the smoke from much heavier artillery fire.

Word came that we were to stop for a break and we drank and ate some sausage and bread. I was shocked to see that it was early afternoon. I would have sworn that we had crossed the Ebro only an hour or two ago, but the day was half done.

We sat and waited for orders for a long time. As we eventually collected our packs and set off again, a squadron of dark shapes flew over, heading toward the river.

"Heinkel one-elevens," Hugh commented, shading his eyes against the sun and squinting up. "Not as fast as those Italian Savoias, but they can carry more bombs. I don't envy the boys working on the river bridges."

We watched them pass in silence. "They were like a flock of big black birds," Bob commented afterward. I didn't reply, but I was glad we had crossed early enough in the morning to miss them.

The rest of the day was spent in a boring march, spread out over the country so as not to offer a tempting target to the planes that shuttled back and forth above us all the time. "Not one of ours," Hugh commented bitterly every time a flight passed over.

I find it hard to believe all the things I have seen today, not just the river crossing or the shell exploding. Almost every moment of today I saw something new and different, and often something dreadful that would *have shocked me into a panic back in the old world. Even on what I called this afternoon's "boring march," I saw bodies, wrecked artillery pieces, a burned-out farmhouse surrounded by dead goats, and groups of our own wounded heading back for the river. The last were filthy, exhausted and bloodstained, and the less severely wounded helped or carried the others, but everyone cheered us as we passed and gave the clenched-fist salute. I wonder if I will be able to go back to worrying about the boring "normal" world after this is all over.*

TWELVE

"Do you think that piece of black metal in the suit-case was the shrapnel that got caught in his pack?"

"Probably," Laia replied. "He seemed to collect things."

"I wish we could know exactly where he was. For all we know, he could have spent the night in that olive grove across the road." We were finishing off a lunch of spicy sausage and bread. At the expense of a wet shirt and Laia's laughter, I was learning how to drink out of a leather *bota*. "At least we're eating and drinking much the same as him."

"When we get to Corbera d'Ebre and Gandesa, it should be easier to work out where things happened." Laia lifted the *bota* and directed a precise stream of water into her mouth from arm's length.

"Corbera can't be far now," I said.

"It's not," Laia agreed, "we'll be there easily by tonight."

"I've been thinking," I said, hesitantly. "Maybe we shouldn't go straight to Corbera."

"What do you mean?" Laia asked. I was relieved to see she looked puzzled at my suggestion and not angry.

"Did you see the map of the area in the display?" She nodded and I hurried on, "It showed a side road going off to a place called La Frat...something."

"La Fatarella," Laia said. I was encouraged to see that she was smiling at my pitiful pronunciation.

"I know my Spanish isn't any good, but there seems to be a museum there, and there was a picture of some trenches."

"Yes," Laia said as she rummaged through the folder of pages she had printed from the Civil War website. "There are a couple of places where the trenches from the fighting are preserved, and you are right, there *is* a museum to the International Brigades in the village itself. We should go there. I am sorry I missed it."

"No, don't be sorry," I said. "You're a great tour guide. I couldn't do this without you."

Laia smiled. "Thank you. There's so much history it's hard to know what to pick. Most of the tourists who come to Spain just come for the sun, the beaches and the cheap wine. They may run through a cathedral, but that's all."

I nodded agreement, thinking of Elsie and Edna from the plane. How was their holiday going? I wondered. Probably very different from mine.

"Only the old people care about our history."

"You care."

"I care because of Maria. You care because of your grandfather."

It was true. History had become much more important to me since reading Grandfather's journal. Maybe that was one thing he intended. "Okay," I said, "let's do it." I stood and stretched my aching back. "Is it far to La Fatarella?"

"Are you regretting our side trip already?" The smile I got from Laia was worth all the discomfort I was certain was soon coming my way.

✿

I groaned at the turnoff when I read the sign announcing that La Fatarella was 8 kilometers away. Then I shook my head in disgust; an aching back and a few kilometers on an uncomfortable scooter were nothing compared to what Grandfather had gone through.

The going was easy for the first couple of kilometers. The road was flat and straight, and there was no traffic. It allowed my mind to wander to something that had been niggling at me for a while. Ultimately we were headed for Corbera, and that was what Grandfather had called the town, but back at the memorial Laia had given it its full name, Corbera d'Ebre, and that was familiar, but from where?

The road was beginning to climb and the scooter's small engine was complaining when I remembered Aina on the bus in from the airport. The town where her grandfather—no, the grandfather of one of her relatives, a cousin or something—lived was Corbera d'Ebre. He had been in the war and been saved by an International Brigader. Aina had given me his address. I tried to reach into my pocket and…almost fell off the scooter. It could wait until we stopped.

I had to concentrate harder on my driving as our route steepened and we began to wind along roads cut between walls of layered white rock. The only buildings were rough stone huts at the edges of the ever-present vineyards and olive groves. Most looked as if they had been there forever and had grown out of the ground rather than been built by farmers.

After a series of particularly vicious switchbacks, the road leveled out as we reached the top of the range of hills. Laia slowed while she checked the map, a feat that would have had me in the ditch. We continued for a few hundred meters and turned off on an unmarked dirt track. After about a hundred meters of wrestling with the scooter as it was mercilessly thrown from one pothole to the next, we stopped beside a pile of rocks. Laia parked her scooter, jumped off and removed her helmet. I followed suit. "Where are we?" I asked.

"Hill five thirty-six," she replied, setting off around the pile of rocks.

All at once, we were standing on the lip of a depression cut out of the hilltop. To one side, a room had been excavated into the rock face; the doorway was surrounded by piled sandbags. Laia scrambled down, and I followed.

"What is this?" I asked as we peered into the dark, dank hole.

"This was part of the trench line that was dug by the Republican soldiers during the battle."

"Could my grandfather have been here?"

Laia thought for a moment. "Probably not. I think these date from November of '38. That was after the International Brigades were sent home."

"They were sent home?" I asked as Laia scrambled around the end of the hollow and up the hill. Then she disappeared.

"Wait," I said, hurrying so much that I slipped and scratched my arm painfully on a sharp rock.

Laia was standing in a trench carved into the rock. It was the scene in the photograph I had found at the memorial. The trench was at least a meter and a half deep and stretched in an irregular line along the crest of the ridge. It was made deeper by rocks roughly placed on the lip. "*Una fosa*," she said. "A trench."

I scrambled down beside her. If I stood up, I could just see over the rocks and across the wide valley at the bottom of the ridge. I tried to imagine being a soldier standing here while the enemy charged up at me. I failed. "This is really from the war?" I asked.

"Yes. People keep it tidy, but this is what it was like."

I walked up and down the short stretch of trench, trying to picture it filled with soldiers: Grandfather, Bob and the others.

"Why were the International Brigades sent home?" I asked once we were back at the scooters.

"The government thought that if they made a gesture, sent home the foreigners who fought for the Republic, that would force Britain and France to put pressure on Germany and Italy to withdraw their troops, planes and tanks. Of course it didn't work, and anyway, I don't think it made any difference. By that time most of the Brigaders had been killed or wounded. Your grandfather says in his journal, even before the Ebro, that most of the men in the Mac-Paps were young Spanish conscripts."

I nodded.

"There was a parade through Barcelona on October 29, 1938. Maria was there. She told me that the streets were covered with flowers and people were weeping openly. La Pasionaria, a Communist politician, made a famous speech to the Brigaders." Laia closed her eyes in concentration. "'You can go with pride. You are history. You are legend. We will not forget you; and, when the olive tree of peace puts forth its leaves, entwined with the laurels of the Spanish Republic's victory, come back!…Long Live the International Brigades.'"

Laia opened her eyes and smiled. "Maria knew the whole speech by heart and, even six decades afterward, could never repeat it without a tear in her eye."

Laia glanced at her watch. "We should probably go if we are to have time to see the museum in La Fatarella before it closes today."

I nodded agreement and hauled my aching limbs onto the scooter.

❖

From the road down the hill into town, La Fatarella looked like a comfortable place, a collection of red-tiled roofs nestled in a curve of the road and surrounded by prosperous farms and regimented terraces of olive groves. With Laia asking directions, we worked our way through the narrow streets, some of which were oddly covered by stone arches and wooden beams, until we arrived at a guesthouse a block away from the church in the center of the village. It was even smaller than our accommodation in Flix, but it was cheap and there was no emotional landlady. We dropped our packs, parked our scooters and walked to the museum of the International Brigades on the edge of town.

The museum wasn't large, but it was packed with information. Dozens of national flags hung to one side and the walls were covered with photographs of soldiers from all around the world who had flocked to fight in Spain.

Laia translated the information boards for me. Of the 40,000 foreigners who volunteered for the International Brigades, the greatest number— 10,000—were from France. The statistics confirmed that almost 1,600 Canadians fought in Spain and that about half of them died.

We spent more than two hours wandering around staring at photographs of stern-looking men and rusted equipment. I tried to imagine Grandfather in the photographs, but it was hard. I knew him when he was alive and I was coming to know him through his writing, but the displays were impersonal and cold. I didn't doubt that the men in the photographs were as passionate as Grandfather, but I didn't know them.

As we stepped out into the late afternoon sunshine, I remembered that there was something I was going to talk to Laia about. "A girl on the bus in from Barcelona airport gave me the address of someone in Corbera. She said he was the grandfather of some relative and that, as a boy, he had been saved by an International Brigader." I reached into my pocket and pulled out the scrap of paper that Aina had given me and handed it to Laia.

"Pablo Aranda, Avinguda Catalunya, 21, 43784, Corbera d'Ebre," she read slowly. "We shall look for him in Corbera. Perhaps he has a story to tell. In any case, you look tired. Perhaps you are not used to our scooters?"

"Not really," I said.

Laia laughed. "Then let us go and find somewhere comfortable to read the next section of the journal, and then we can find some dinner."

"Sounds good, but first I have to call home to let Mom know I am all right. This would be a good time to catch her."

Laia moved away from me as I took out my phone. I had a couple of texts from DJ. Getting up, but it's hard, the first one read. I never thought I could be this tired. The second one said simply, Hope I can make it. That wasn't like DJ. It worried me. I texted back, Go for it. I wanted to say more but I was confused by DJ's uncertainty.

The phone call to Mom went well. I told her I was fine and had found out a lot about Grandfather, without going into specifics. She told me stuff that was going on at home, none of which seemed in the least bit important in the middle of my adventure.

I felt odd as I folded the phone. Toronto was dull compared to what Grandfather had gone through and even compared to what I was doing.

"Your mother is well?" Laia asked.

"Fine," I replied.

"Let's read the next chapter then."

JULY 26, AFTERNOON

Sitting on a hill outside Corbera watching the town being pounded by wave after wave of bombers. Most come over at high altitude—3,000 feet Hugh says. I am learning to recognize the sleek gull-winged Heinkels and the ugly three-engined Savoias.

The noise is terrifying, great successions of explosions as the sticks of bombs explode in a line. It's like rolling thunder but harsher. Between the explosions, we can make out the crash of collapsing buildings and, even across the valley, the screams of the wounded and trapped. The entire hilltop is mostly invisible behind a swirling, dirty cloud of smoke and dust. As many of the inhabitants as possible have fled into the olive groves in the surrounding fields, and we can see their tiny black shapes. Some bombs have hit the dam that held back the town's reservoir, and a wall of water cascaded down the road. I hope no one was in the way.

The Poles of the Dabrowski Battalion took the town this morning, but they have pulled back because of the bombing. The Catalans we have been following for two days are almost at Gandesa, 3 miles farther on, and we are to take over from them tomorrow in preparation for the attack on that place. Everything is going well and we have taken a lot of territory, although some units have suffered heavily and resistance appears to be solidifying. Tiny says that once Gandesa is ours, the Fascists will find it very difficult to move troops and supplies around because it is a major road junction. I wish our tanks would hurry and show up. At least our air force has put in an appearance.

This morning we were attacked by a German fighter plane. According to Hugh, who seems to know everything about the enemy equipment, it was a Messerschmitt 109, one of the most advanced fighters in the world and more than a match for anything Britain or France has. It came in low over a hill while we were marching in loose formation across open ground. The first we knew was when bullets began kicking up the dirt around us. It was a pale-gray machine with the Fascist black diagonal cross on the tail, and it made three passes, although no one was wounded.

It was swinging round for a fourth pass when three of our Chatos appeared from the north and engaged it. We all leaped to our feet and cheered wildly as the shapes twisted and turned frantically above us.

The Messerschmitt was faster, but the Chatos turned tightly and one of them must have got in a lucky shot as the Fascist plane turned away toward the river, trailing a long black stream of smoke. The Chatos didn't follow, but they waggled their wings over us in greeting and we all cheered until we were hoarse. Now all we need are the tanks and there will be no stopping us.

JULY 26, EVENING

We are in Corbera, or rather what's left of it. It is built around a church on a hilltop, but mostly all that is left are the smoking shells of buildings and rubble-filled streets. There are ripped drapes, shattered furniture and smouldering bedding everywhere, and fires are still burning in some streets. There are bodies among the collapsed walls, but most of the injured have been moved to a first-aid station set up in what is left of the town winery. Those who fled the bombing are staying overnight in the surrounding olive groves in case the bombers return.

Our squad was among the first in after the bombing stopped, and we have been working steadily since to search for and rescue those trapped in the ruins. Most of those we found were dead or dying, but there was one shining moment.

We were passing a collapsed house when Bob stopped and ordered us all to be quiet. Very faintly, we could hear a child crying. Following the sound and working very slowly and carefully, we eventually located where it was coming from. When the house had collapsed, one of the roof beams had fallen and created a small space in the corner of one room. A child, a boy of about six or seven, was huddled under the beam. He was scratched and scared, but suffered nothing worse. Tiny, in an incredible feat of strength, lifted the beam high enough for Bob to reach in and pull the kid out.

We were convinced that the child's family had been killed in the house and were taking him to the first-aid station when he abruptly broke free from Bob's arms and ran across the street shouting "Mama" at the top of his voice. A young woman sitting on a pile of rubble looked up and screamed. She was the child's mother and was convinced that her son was dead. It felt good to save a life and reunite a family amid all this death and destruction.

The worst thing is how impersonal everything is. I expected to be fighting against other people, but it is like battling against a vast uncaring machine. We see the planes that drop the bombs, but not the pilots. We don't even see the artillery that lobs shells at us from over the farthest range of hills. How can we fight back against that? I want to see the enemy.

Or do I? We will attack Gandesa tomorrow or the next day, with or without the tanks. Will it succeed or fail? Will I survive? What friends will I lose?

I still feel passionate about the cause I came to fight for, it's just that there is a difference between the grand idea, which is admirable, and the way it must be achieved, which involves incalculable pain and suffering. Is it worth it? My first instinct is, yes, of course it is worth it. The Fascists must be defeated. But could I justify our battle to that mother if Bob had not heard her boy crying and he had died in that ruined house? I don't know.

All of a sudden, things seem so bleak and compli-cated. I'm tired. I must try and get some sleep.

THIRTEEN

The whine of falling bombs, the crash of exploding shells, planes roaring overhead, tanks rumbling past and men shouting. The sensations were overwhelming. The only thing missing was the danger.

Laia and I were standing with our eyes closed in the introductory section of the Museum of 115 Days in Corbera, trying to imagine what it must have been like for Grandfather hearing these noises.

I had woken up stiff and sore that morning, and the scooter ride from La Fatarella to Corbera hadn't improved things. But being here had completely re-energized me. Being in Corbera and hearing the sounds in the museum was as close as I could possibly get to living the things that Grandfather was talking about in his journal.

The old town on the hill that he had witnessed bombed to rubble had been preserved exactly as it was the day he was there. Rubble had been cleared from the open areas and weeds had taken over the streets and alleys, but the church, its walls pock-marked by shells and bullets, still stood, surrounded by the stark ruined stone walls of houses. Fire-blackened beams, possibly even the one that Tiny had lifted, poked up from collapsed walls. Oddly, in one house, a rusted, old-fashioned sewing machine sat alone on top of a pile of stones.

Laia and I had the place to ourselves, and we wandered round in silence, trying to imagine the horror and chaos the destroyed houses represented. I found myself staring into the corners of ruins, wondering if this was where the boy Bob saved had been trapped. I couldn't get what Grandfather had said out of my mind. I was as convinced as he had been that the cause he had fought for was just. But was even a just cause worth all the suffering? Was it even worth the life of that one boy? I wondered if Grandfather had found the answer to his questions. I certainly hadn't found the answers to mine.

Now we were in the museum in the new town at the bottom of the hill, named for the 115 days the Battle of the Ebro lasted, listening to the noises of that horror.

"It's hard to imagine what your grandfather— what all the soldiers—went through," Laia said as we moved among display cases of old uniforms, helmets, shells, bombs and guns. "Maria talked about the fighting in the streets of Barcelona. I understood what she was saying, but I never felt it the way I have among the ruined houses here or in the trenches outside La Fatarella. Even so, I can't imagine what it was like in the middle of all the things he talks about. Why do people go to war?"

"With Grandfather," I said slowly as I thought about each word, "and probably with Bob and the others, it was for something that they believed in. I think they were trying to make the world a better place."

"Yes," Laia said as we stared at a case full of evil-looking bombs and rockets, "but he had doubts about whether it was worth it."

"I know, but we know things he didn't. Maybe if Grandfather and the others had won in Spain, if Canada and the other democracies had got their act together and beaten the Fascists in 1936, there wouldn't have been a Second World War— no Hiroshima, no Holocaust, millions of lives saved. I've always thought history was simple, but it's not. It's complicated."

"It is," Laia agreed. "I think we will go crazy if we try to work out answers. Nobody has in thousands of years of history, so I doubt we will. All we can do is follow your grandfather's journal and see where it leads us."

We examined the rest of the exhibits in silence. It was late afternoon by the time we finished, and I didn't feel like going to find the address Aina had given me. Since neither of us had eaten lunch, we went in search of a meal instead, returned to the guesthouse we had signed into that morning and settled down with the journal. I had a growing feeling that Grandfather's story was building to some kind of crisis, and I was eager to continue.

JULY 27, NOON

A short break after a hard morning's march to these low hills overlooking Gandesa and then two hours scraping a shallow trench in this rocky ground. We have piled a line of rocks on the lip of our ditch (it's not really deep enough to call it a trench), and that gives us a bit more cover, but Tiny still has to crawl everywhere on his hands and knees. Not that anyone is firing at us. There is a steady stream of planes overhead, but they are high and don't pay us any mind. The odd artillery shell explodes on the hill, but the rounds are not aimed and do little damage. Besides, we shall not be here long. Word is, the tanks have got across the river and will be here tomorrow morning to support our attack on Gandesa.

I can see the edge of town from here. Our artillery in the hills is firing, and puffs of gray smoke and dust show where our shells land. It looks harmless from this distance, but I hope our barrage is doing damage.

The plain in front of Gandesa is wide and flat, ideal for tanks, Hugh says. I hope so.

The plan is that the XVth Brigade will move into the valley under cover of darkness and attack at dawn, sweeping through the streets before the defenders *have time to organize. Other troops will attack other parts of the city. With the tanks, and hopefully planes, we will succeed. It's the waiting that's hard.*

JULY 27, AFTERNOON

One of the Americans is dead and another wounded. We were resting in whatever shade we could find when Hugh yelled a warning. "Dive-bombers!"

He dove past me into our ditch, and I followed without really knowing what was happening. Others were running here and there, but the three Americans simply stood up, sheltered their eyes and stared at the sky. I looked up as well. At first it looked like the view we had seen all day—flights of aircraft heading over toward the river—but then I noticed that some of the aircraft were different. They were smaller than the Heinkels and Savoias, were flying lower and had odd bent wings.

There were five of them, and they were almost directly overhead when the lead plane peeled off and plummeted straight down. The others followed. Hugh had been right earlier when he said it seemed as if they were aiming straight for you. They looked like evil, black birds with their bent wings and fixed under-carriages, and they made an unearthly wailing sound.

There was something hideously fascinating about them. As I watched the lead plane fall toward me, I began to wonder if this was some kind of suicide attack, but at the last minute the plane pulled out of its dive. A tiny black object wobbled down from the plane's belly. I knew what that was, so I rolled onto my side, drew my knees up to my chest and covered the back of my head with my arms.

I could see the Americans, as enthralled by the planes as I was but standing in the open beside an ancient olive tree. I wanted to yell at them to lie down, but the plane's siren drowned everything.

The bomb landed no more than 7 feet away from the men. The closest man was picked up like a rag doll and flung into the branches of the olive tree; the second man was thrown violently down and to one side; and the third, Carl the taxi driver, remained standing, protected from the blast by the tree trunk.

It was all over in seconds. Other bombs exploded along the hillside, and after the noise died away, I heard screams coming from my left. I was first on my feet, heading for the wounded men, not thinking that the planes might come back for a second run.

The man in the tree was bent over at an impossible angle and obviously dead. His companion on the ground didn't look too bad but was groaning pitifully and holding his stomach. Carl was standing, staring blankly, as I knelt beside the wounded man. I yelled at Carl to come and help. He didn't move. Then Tiny was there taking charge. He lifted the man's hands off his stomach to reveal a rapidly spreading red stain. "Stomach wound," he said. "Don't touch him," he added, looking at me. "Hugh, get a stretcher up here."

Hugh disappeared through the trees, and Tiny stood and went over to Carl. "You'll be all right," I said to the man on the ground. He struggled to focus on me. His teeth were chattering. "I'm cold," he said. I went and got a blanket and draped it over him. He didn't seem to notice.

Hugh arrived back with a couple of Spaniards and a stretcher. As gently as possible, we loaded the man onto it, and they headed off toward the aid station. Tiny came back over and Hugh looked up at him and shook his head. Tiny nodded. "Get that body out of the tree," he ordered. I stood up, but Marcel and Christopher were already working on it. I looked over at Carl.

He was in exactly the same position as before, a vacant stare on his face.

"Are you okay?" I asked, moving over beside him. There was no response. I tugged his arm and he slowly turned his head, swallowed and blinked rapidly a few times. He looked around and his brow furrowed in puzzlement. "What happened?" he asked.

"We were bombed," I said. He nodded as if that explained everything.

Tiny came over and put a massive arm around Carl's shoulder. "It's shock," he said to me. "He'll be okay with a bit of rest."

Tiny led Carl away, and I went back to our ditch, wondering where Carl was going to get some rest in the middle of a battle. We had lost three of our small group already, four if Carl didn't recover. That only left Tiny, Hugh, Marcel, Christopher, me and Bob.

Bob! Where was he? I stood up and was relieved to see him coming through the trees with an armful of sticks. "I thought a fire might be a good idea," he said as he reached me and dropped his bundle. "Make some tea and heat up some sausage stew. We can't go into battle on an empty stomach."

"Don't you know what happened?"

"I know there was an air raid. I heard the explosions. Stukas, some fellow along the hill told me. Why?"

"One of the bombs landed here, right beside the Americans. One was killed, another badly wounded. Carl wasn't hurt, but he's in shock."

Bob's good mood evaporated. "Damn," he said. "There goes our good luck. One dead and two wounded before we even go into battle."

We lapsed into silence and sat with our own thoughts. I couldn't get rid of the images of Carl's empty eyes and the American with a piece of shrapnel in his stomach, shivering and complaining of the cold. Is that the sort of thing that's waiting for all of us?

JULY 27, EVENING

I cannot live through many more afternoons like this—first the bombing and now I think I have killed a man.

I was crouched in the pitiful trench I scooped out this morning when I saw a movement on the rocky hillside across the valley. It was a man—a Fascist soldier—in a much neater uniform than the rags many of us wear. I watched him for some time as he scrambled from rock to rock on the otherwise bare hill.

I had no idea why he was crossing the exposed hillside. As far as I could see, there were no Fascist trenches over there. Perhaps he was lost, separated from his unit as they retreated to Gandesa yesterday. He seemed to be alone. I followed his progress along the barrel of my rifle, wondering what to do. He was heading for a narrow ravine. If he made it, he would be hidden and able to work his way down the valley into Gandesa. When we attack the town tomorrow, it might be him aiming a rifle at me.

I made my decision and guessed where he would appear next. When he broke from cover, I remembered what Tiny had taught me, and I aimed a couple of feet ahead of his running form and squeezed the trigger. The man stumbled, dropped his rifle and fell behind a large rock. I waited for an age, but he didn't try to retrieve his rifle or continue his journey on the other side of his shelter.

Did I kill him or was he playing safe after hearing my bullet zing by? I don't know, but it is the first time I have deliberately tried to kill someone I can clearly see, and it feels odd. He was not an invisible bomber pilot or unseen artillery man. He was a human being.

Bob said I did right. He said we came here to do just that, kill the men who are trying to destroy everything good in Spain. He said everything we do here is a blow against Adrian Arcand's Fascists marching through the streets of Montreal, smashing shop windows and beating up any Jews they find. I know Bob's right. I also know the man on the hillside would have killed me if he had a chance, but I also know what a bullet can do to flesh and bone, and I can't help wondering whether the man I might have shot had a mother who will mourn him or children who will never see their father again.

I helped save a life yesterday, and today I might have taken one. None of this is what I wanted when I came here. But what did I expect? I was a stupid kid with no idea. What did I think, that wars are fought without blood and death, like a story in the Boy's Own Annual? Did I really imagine that men don't scream when a piece of a bomb tears a hole in them? I don't know if I will be able to force myself to go down into Gandesa tomorrow.

I must try and put these thoughts from my mind. I need to sleep. But I won't; I can hear the drone of the bombers approaching again.

FOURTEEN

I woke up the next morning feeling dragged out. It had been a restless night's sleep, filled with dreams of fighting and death. Over a breakfast coffee and pastry, Laia admitted that she had not slept well either.

"There is not much of the journal left, and I don't think it is going to be happy," she said, mirroring my sense of foreboding.

"Maybe it won't be too bad," I said without much conviction. "Perhaps the tanks will help and they will capture the town."

Laia gave me a long look.

"They fail, don't they?"

Laia nodded. "Gandesa was never captured."

We sat in silence. It felt very strange. I had been living the journal as I read it. I was with Grandfather as he struggled along, watching his friends being killed. I felt his shock at shooting the man on the hillside. It was all so real, and it was going to go horribly wrong. I wanted to shout a warning to him—and Bob, Tiny, Hugh, Marcel, Christopher and Carl.

Don't do it.

It won't work.

Don't go on the attack tomorrow.

But of course that was crazy. The things I was reading about had happened more than seventy years ago. I couldn't change the outcome.

"Let's go to the address that Aina gave you on the bus," Laia suggested. "What was the name?"

I retrieved the scrap of paper from my pocket. "Pablo Aranda, but he doesn't have anything to do with Grandfather's story."

"Probably not, but Aina told you he was rescued by an International Brigader. What if this Pablo is the boy who Bob and Tiny rescued from the ruined house? This is a small town. How many boys were rescued from ruined houses?"

"I've wondered about that. I don't know. It's quite a coincidence. We know that Pablo Aranda lives here now, but Aina never said this was where he was rescued or even if it had happened in '38. There must have been a lot of incidents like that in the war."

"True," Laia acknowledged, "but you never know. Besides, we're here and what harm can it do?"

"Okay," I agreed. At least it gave me an excuse to postpone reading the last few pages of the journal, which I was both looking forward to and dreading.

It only took us a few minutes to find Avinguda Catalunya, 21. It was a door covered in peeling red paint, in the wall beside a *Farmacia*. Laia rang the bell. For a long time nothing happened and we were about to leave, when I heard slow footsteps descending the stairs. The door creaked open to reveal an old man leaning on a cane.

"Pablo Aranda?" Laia asked.

The old man frowned but nodded slowly. Laia introduced us both, explained that we had been given his name and address by Aina and wished to talk about the war.

"*No hablo de la guerra*," the old man grunted and began to close the door.

"My friend, Esteban, has come all the way from Canada to hear about the war," Laia explained.

The old man stopped and stared at me. Despite his age, he stood straight and held his head high. The skin of his face was wrinkled and weather-beaten, but his eyes were sharp and peered hard from either side of a hawklike nose. "You are from Canada?" he asked, switching to heavily accented English.

"I am," I said.

The man continued to stare at me. Before I could think of anything else to say, Laia spoke. "You were rescued by a Canadian during the war."

Both the old man and I swiveled our heads and gazed at Laia as she continued. "We know a boy was rescued from a ruined house here by a Canadian during the battle in 1938. That was you, wasn't it?"

The old man looked long at Laia before returning his stare to me. "*Pasen.*" Follow me. He made it sound like a military order. Then he turned and clumped slowly up the long flight of stairs. Laia caught my eye and winked broadly.

The room that Pablo Aranda led us into was sparsely furnished, but the walls were covered with black-and-white photographs. Some were obviously family shots, but others showed businessmen in suits and ties, and several were of soldiers. I didn't have time to examine them in any detail. There was an empty coffee cup and a half-eaten pastry on the coffee table, but Aranda didn't offer us anything, merely grunting and waving an arm toward a worn couch.

We sat and the old man settled into the armchair opposite and regarded us with a stony stare. "As a boy you were rescued by a Canadian?" Laia asked encouragingly.

"*Sí*," Aranda said.

"Here in Corbera d'Ebre?" Laia asked when Aranda didn't contribute anything else.

Aranda didn't answer for a long time. He seemed to be considering something at length, and Laia and I waited. Eventually, he sighed and began speaking. He spoke in halting English laced with Spanish expressions when he couldn't think of the right word, but we listened patiently and, with some help from Laia, his story emerged.

"Yes. I was"—he held up a hand spread open—"*cinco años* when the *aviones*, the planes, came. *Los Comunistas* were in Corbera, and *mi madre*, my mother, and I hide in our house." Aranda glanced up at a photograph on the wall behind us before continuing. "*Mi padre* was away at war."

Laia turned and looked at the picture. I felt her tense, but she said nothing.

"*Estalló la primera bomba.*" Aranda furrowed his brow in concentration.

"The first bomb exploded," Laia said.

"*Sí.*" Aranda nodded. "The first bomb exploded"— he glanced at the window—"outside. My mother, she was in kitchen. I was in bed. I hid…" Aranda made a scooping motion with his hand.

"Under the bed?" I suggested.

Aranda nodded. "I live because I hid. *La segunda*, the second bomb, exploded in kitchen. My mother flew through the window. She awoke in *la calle*, the street. I only knew the noise—*muy ruidoso.*"

"Very loud," Laia translated.

Aranda nodded again. "Next, I lay in the dark. There was heavy—something heavy on my legs. My *oídos*—" He touched the side of his head and looked at Laia.

"Ears," she said.

"*Sí*, ears. It was like the sea roaring. I was dead, I thought. Much time went on. *Grité*—"

"You cried out."

"Yes, cried out. Next there was a giant lifting the heaviness."

"Tiny," I blurted out.

Aranda glanced at me and continued. "A soldier pulled me and carried me outside. He say, '*Soy Canadiense*,' many, many time. I saw my mother."

Aranda appeared to have finished his story. He sat back and looked at us. "He must be the boy that Tiny and Bob rescued," I said to Laia.

"It seems so," she replied quietly. I was puzzled; she didn't seem nearly as excited at our discovery as I felt. She turned to Aranda and spoke rapidly in Spanish. I caught the names *Tiny* and *Bob* and assumed she was telling him our part of the tale. Aranda watched her without expression, occasionally glancing at me. Laia finished with a question, and Aranda nodded and said, "*Sí.*"

When she had finished, she said me, "I told him the story from your grandfather's journal. I described them and told him the date. I asked him if he thinks Tiny and Bob were the ones who saved him. He does."

"This is incredible," I said, thrilled at discovering a living link to my grandfather's adventures. "We must ask him more about what happened here."

"I don't think so," Laia said. Before I had a chance to ask what she meant, she turned back to Aranda. "*Sobrevivió la guerra su padre?*"

Again Aranda nodded. "*Sí. Fue alcalde de Corbera.*"

Laia translated, "I asked him if his father survived the war. He said he did and that he became mayor of Corbera."

"That's great," I enthused. "He did well."

Laia looked at me for a long time before she spoke. "After General Franco won the war, he began a campaign to cleanse Spain of all undesirable elements. Any Socialists, Communists or Anarchists were shot. I showed you the wall of Sant Felip

Neri church in Barcelona where people were shot.
Many thousands of people, some say hundreds of
thousands, were shot after the war. Mass graves have
been found all over Spain."

"That's tragic," I said, "but why are you telling
me this now?"

Laia swiveled round and pointed to a large framed
photograph on the wall behind us. It showed a crowd
of soldiers standing in front of a church. There were
two men in the foreground, shaking hands, both
dressed in smart uniforms. "Do you recognize the
man on the right?" Laia asked.

"Yes. It's General Franco."

"Yes, and the other man is the mayor of Corbera,
Pablo Aranda's father."

As the importance of this was sinking in, Laia
went on. "After the war those who had helped
Franco win it were given positions of power—
judges, police captains"—she hesitated—"and
mayors. It was their job to weed out the undesir-
ables in their town or neighborhood, those who had
fought for the Republic, been active in the trade
unions or against whom they simply had a grudge,
and deal with them."

A chill ran down my spine as the meaning of what I was being told sank in. I looked back at Aranda. He was sitting calmly watching me. "Your father was a Fascist?" I asked.

Aranda nodded slowly. "Your *abuelo*—" He glanced at Laia.

"Grandfather," she translated.

"Your grandfather was a Communist?"

"But he was fighting for the Republic. He fought for what was right," I said indignantly.

Aranda threw his head back and let out a coarse laugh. When he looked back, he was smiling. "'He fought for what was right,'" he mimicked, bitterly. "The sister of my father, *mi tía*, lived in Barcelona. She was *muy pequeña*." He held his hand out to one side to show how short his aunt was. "She was a woman of God, a nun. My first remembrance, I was *tres años*, three years in age, was a visit to her *convento*. She gave me *caramelos*." Aranda lifted a hand to his mouth and kissed his fingertips with a loud smacking noise. "They were *delicioso*. I thought, this is an *ángel* and this is what paradise is like."

Both Laia and I sat silent. As the old man talked, his smile faded. "When *la guerra*, the war, began, *los anarquistas* burned the little church of *mi tía*. But first, they took rope and tied *mi tía* and eleven others to *el crucifijo*, the crucifix. All burned to death."

Aranda's eyes filled with tears, and he lowered his head. He looked sad and old. "That's horrible," I said.

Aranda's head snapped up. He blinked rapidly and the hard expression he had welcomed us with returned to his face. "He fought for what was right," he repeated, his voice ugly with sarcasm. "My father fought for right. For God. For Spain. I am *agradecido*." He flashed a look at Laia. "Grateful," she translated.

"I am grateful for your grandfather and his *amigos*, for aiding me. But they were wrong." Aranda stood up, stiffly. "Now you must go. You have disturbed too much past."

Laia and I mumbled our thanks and retreated down the stairs and onto the bright street in silence. Without discussing where we were going, we walked back up to the ruined old town. We sat down in the sun with our backs to the old church wall.

I guess I had assumed that everyone today knew that the Republic had been right and the Fascists evil, that the volunteers had fought for something just and right while the rest of the world betrayed them.

"It wasn't simple," Laia said as if reading my thoughts. "It isn't simple. Both sides of the war live on in Spain today. Many people miss the stability that Franco's dictatorship gave them. I told you before: you can't escape history. And history isn't good or bad; it simply is. Dreadful things happen in war, on both sides. I think your grandfather was beginning to realize that when he shot the soldier on the hillside."

I sat and thought for a long time. Laia was right, and I had been naïve to believe that something as complicated as a war could be a simple question of black and white. One side being right didn't mean there couldn't be evil and tragedy on both sides.

I took the journal out of my pack and opened it. Laia started to stand up. "No," I said, "let's read it together."

JULY 28, MORNING

Where are the tanks? They were supposed to be here early so we could attack at dawn, but the sun's well up and there's no sign of them. Everybody is tense.

We came down from the hills in the dark, and now we're spread out through an olive grove. I can see the houses on the edge of Gandesa across a wide stretch of flat farmland. There are figures darting between the houses, but it looks quiet. Occasionally, shells whine overhead from our artillery back up on the hills and explode in the town with muffled crumps and clouds of smoke and brick dust. I can hear more explosions and the crackle of rifle and machine-gun fire from the far side of town. I hope that keeps the enemy busy when it's our turn to attack. Where are the tanks?

Planes continually fly overhead, but they are all Fascist and all heading for the river. I commented to Hugh that it would be nice if we had some planes here, and he said it would make no difference, they would be shot out of the sky like every other time. He pointed out the long barrel of a gun pointing at the sky between two buildings in Gandesa. "That's an eighty-eight," he said. "A new German anti-aircraft gun. I suspect it would simply pick our little air force out of the sky one by one."

It's odd how the seven of us left in the squad handle the tension. We tried to leave Carl back up on the hill—he's obviously still in shock—but the commissar insisted he be brought down for the attack. He even threatened to shoot him for desertion if we left him. So we brought him, although there are times when he merely sits and stares wide-eyed at the ground between his feet, completely unaware of where he is.

I write in these pages to calm myself. Bob sings quietly. He has a good voice, but I think if I hear "Red River Valley" once more, I will shoot him myself. Christopher reads a small volume of poetry he carries everywhere with him. It's by an English poet called Keats. Marcel and Hugh argue about everything, from how incompetent the generals were in the Great War, to the subtleties of socialist philosophy. Tiny flits between us, asking how each of us is and checking that our weapons are clean and ready.

I am amazed that it is only six weeks since I crossed the mountains. I look back at the pages I wrote then and they seem to be by someone else. Someone much younger and more naïve. Would I still have come here had I known what was in store for me in those six weeks?

Yes, for two reasons. What I am fighting for is right. It is not as simple as I thought, but it is still right.

The second reason is the nurse in Barcelona. I cannot get her out of my mind. I only met her very *briefly and we only exchanged a few words, but I dream of her eyes. Perhaps it is only the loneliness and the fear of the past few days, but I will find her when I return to Barcelona and tell her how I feel.*

I must stop now, there is rumbling behind me. It must be our tanks. We are ordered to leave our packs, so I will carry this journal in my breast pocket. Its fate will be mine.

JULY 28, EVENING

The first word is the hardest to write, and I have sat and stared at this blank page for an age. Had I not promised to fill this book, I would write nothing. It is too painful. However, I did promise and I have begun, so I shall take a deep breath and continue.

Bob and I are in a gloomy barn filled with wounded men, awaiting an ambulance to take us to the train back to Barcelona. The place smells of blood and death, an odd, sweet smell. It is an antechamber to Hell. The wounded lie in rows along each wall, the lucky ones with some filthy straw between them and the hard ground. Some are missing arms or legs. The faces of others are hidden behind bloodstained rags. One man with a stomach wound has died already, and his body was carried outside. Most are silent, although some whimper quietly, and I shudder at the occasional scream.

There is one man who calls himself a doctor, but he does nothing other than mumble a few words of comfort and offer water to drink. Not that there is much he could do since there are no medicines, bandages or nurses to help him.

Bob has a piece of shrapnel in his shoulder. The wound bled a lot—that is his blood on the cover of my journal—but it's not too serious. At first he lost the use of his left arm, but already the feeling is returning to his fingers. Unless some incompetent doctor causes more damage digging for the piece of metal that is still in there, he should heal.

I have a bruise the size of a basketball on the left side of my chest and, I suspect, several broken ribs. I can only breathe very shallow, and coughing is agony. One ambulance has been already, but it took the most serious cases. I suspect Bob and I will be here for some time.

Why are conditions so bad? Did they expect there to be a battle without casualties? Is there really nothing to give us, or is it simply bad organization?

Hugh would say the latter. But then, Hugh will never say anything again. Bob and I are all that remain from our squad and I am searching for things to write about to postpone going back to tell the story of this terrible day.

The tanks arrived this morning, five squat things that rattled and clanked along between the trees. Orders were shouted, and they pushed on out into the open. We followed with high hopes, although Carl soon fell behind and I never saw him again.

At first all went well. The Fascist fire was not heavy, and the bullets either zinged overhead or pinged off the tanks' armor plate. Then the lead tank, off to my right, exploded. The turret cartwheeled off, and a ball of flame rose from the gaping hole.

I looked at Gandesa and saw that the barrel of the anti-aircraft gun that Hugh had pointed out earlier was now horizontal. I saw a flash, and a column of dust rose beside another tank. Not every shot counted, but the gun fired rapidly and every hit went through our tanks' armor plate like it was paper. It was like a training exercise for the German gunners. Marcel died when the tank near him blew and a heavy piece of metal caught him in the head.

The machine guns opened up when we were about halfway over and the last tank had been destroyed. Some men had bunched up behind the tanks, and they suffered badly. Our squad was more spread out, and we were three-quarters of the way over before we were targeted.

"Down!" Tiny yelled.

When the machine gun moved on, he ordered, "Up!"

Between his orders, I either lay still or moved forward in a stumbling run. Oddly, I was much less frightened with men being killed and wounded all around me than I had been waiting for the tanks to arrive. Rationally, I knew what was happening and that I was in great danger, yet it was as if I was watching everything from a distance. Even when Christopher was too slow getting down and a line of bullets caught him across the chest, my mind simply recorded the fact and I felt no sorrow. It was as if I had given up all responsibility for my existence to Tiny and, as long as I did what he told me, I would be all right.

We progressed like automatons, concentrating only on Tiny's orders and obeying them. Miraculously, we were suddenly at the buildings on the edge of Gandesa. I caught a glimpse of figures running through the streets ahead of me but didn't have time to get off a shot.

Tiny yelled at Hugh, who lobbed a grenade through the nearest open window while the rest of us crouched against the wall. The explosion shook the ground, and then Tiny kicked in the door and disappeared. Hugh, Bob and I followed. The room was filled with smoke and ruined furniture but otherwise empty. We cleared the other rooms and paused, listening to other brigaders working their way through the houses on either side of us.

"Well, we're in Gandesa," Tiny said, peering out the doorway and down the street. "Anybody see what happened to Carl?" The three of us shook our heads.

"A lot of use the tanks were," Hugh said. "Those eighty-eight shells didn't even slow down when they hit them."

"Glad I wasn't inside one," Bob offered.

"They wouldn't be much use in these narrow streets anyway," Tiny added. "I wonder how many of us made it across those open fields."

"Not enough," Hugh said.

"Well, some did," Tiny pointed out. "Hear all that fighting around us? I guess we'd better press on as far as we can. Take a drink and make sure you've got a full clip in your rifle."

At the mention of taking a drink, I suddenly realized how dry my mouth was. I drank greedily. Then I checked my rifle and was surprised to find I hadn't fired a shot on the way over. The safety clip was still on. Sheepishly, I flicked it off.

"Good idea," Bob said quietly.

"Come on then, you lazy lot," Tiny said, heading for the door. "There's work to be done."

I was just passing the window when I saw the building across the street collapse with a deafening roar. It felt as if a huge hand picked me up and flung me against the wall on the other side of the room. "What happened?" I asked, getting unsteadily to my feet and checking that nothing was broken.

"Artillery shell," Tiny explained.

"Ours or theirs?" Hugh asked.

Tiny shrugged. "Doesn't matter. What matters is that we get moving before the next one comes over. You all right?" he asked me. I nodded. Tiny headed for the door. "At least the smoke will give us a bit of cover. Hugh and I'll go up this side of the street. You two go up the other. Keep pace with us, keep your eyes open and hug the wall like you love it."

Tiny looked up and down the street and slipped out, followed quickly by Hugh. "I guess we'd better go," Bob said. "You up for it?"

"Yes," I said as he, too, slipped out the door and sprinted across the street. I followed, avoiding the rubble from the collapsed house. We progressed slowly, carefully checking every door and window as we went. It was nerve-racking work and our progress was painfully slow. Rifle and machine-gun fire and the crump of grenades echoed from the streets round about us, becoming heavier as we advanced.

We had checked three houses when a group of figures burst out of a side alley. Instinctively, we raised our weapons, but they were brigaders. An officer approached Tiny. "They're counterattacking on both sides," he explained. "There's not enough of us to hold. We're withdrawing."

"Withdrawing?" Tiny said, looking down the street in front of us. "There's no resistance here. We can keep going."

"If we do that, we'll be cut off. Not enough of us made it across the open, and some of my men are running out of ammunition already. We've no grenades."

Tiny hesitated, gave one last glance down the empty street leading into town, and turned back. He looked across at Bob and me and opened his mouth. Then he hesitated. A puzzled frown crossed his face and he slowly sank to his knees. A bullet chipped the wall behind him and whined off into the air.

"Sniper!" the officer yelled, pointing up the street. Bob and I followed the line of his arm. "In that church bell tower."

I couldn't see anything, but I loosed off a couple of shots at the tower. So did Bob. Already, Hugh had his hands under Tiny's arms and was dragging him back down the street. Firing as we went to keep the sniper's head down, we retreated to the first house we had cleared.

Breathing heavily, Hugh leaned Tiny against a wall. The big man was breathing irregularly through his mouth and looked frighteningly pale. "I can't feel my legs," he said weakly.

"They're coming down the street," a man at the window shouted. I peered out the doorway. Figures in red hats were working slowly down either side of the street. The soldier in the window and I got off a couple of shots. One figure crumpled to the ground, and the others disappeared into doorways. Bullets began to chip the walls around us.

"We can't stay here," the officer shouted. Hugh began to lift Tiny.

"Leave him."

"No way," Hugh replied. "You know what the Fascists do to prisoners."

"He's too big. He'll slow us down. You can't carry him."

"Yes, we can," Bob said, slinging his rifle over his shoulder. He helped Hugh lift Tiny.

"Suit yourselves," the officer said. "Come on." He and his men disappeared onto the street, firing as they went.

Bob and Hugh had Tiny between them. "Keep the Fascist heads down," Hugh told me as they headed for the door.

That's how we progressed, changing places frequently, but always two of us hauling Tiny and one firing back. Tiny grunted at first at the manhandling but soon just gritted his teeth in silence.

The open fields were filled with men stumbling back from the town. At first the fire on our backs from the town wasn't heavy as the Fascists advanced carefully, checking the buildings as they went, but it increased as we stumbled along.

Bob and I were hauling Tiny when the artillery opened up and shells began exploding around us.

Suddenly I was carrying Tiny on my own. His weight was too much and we collapsed in a heap, Tiny grunting with the pain.

Bob was crouched nearby, his knees drawn up to his chest and his arms crossed on his chest, his fists balled tightly. I crawled over. "Where are you hit?" *I asked. Bob simply whimpered. I checked him over as best I could but could find nothing. I shook him.* "Bob, what happened?"

He looked over at me, his eyes wide and snot running from his nose. "I can't go on," *he whimpered.*

"Of course you can," *I said, trying to haul him to his feet.*

He resisted. "I can't," *he repeated.* "It's too much. Don't make me."

Hugh appeared beside us. "What's happening? Is he hit?"

"I don't think so. He just won't move."

"Then leave him. We've got to get Tiny back."

"No," *I said.* "You go on if you want, but I'm not leaving Bob."

I turned to my friend. "It's okay, Bob, but it's not just you and me. It's Tiny—he's badly hurt, and I can't get him back on my own. I need you to help me."

Bob looked at me and blinked rapidly. "Tiny?" he said.

"Yes, Tiny. He's wounded and you have to help me. Will you?"

Slowly, Bob got to his feet. I kept talking to keep him going. "We're almost at the trees. We can rest there." Hugh and I lifted Tiny and draped an arm across Bob's shoulder. I took the other side. "Okay, Bob?" I asked, shouting above the explosions and whining bullets.

"Okay," Bob shouted back. We set off at a slow stagger. It was hard going, but we kept on. Then the dive-bombers returned, announced by the terrifying whine as they plunged toward us.

I glanced back over my shoulder to see Hugh firing his rifle in the air. The bomb must have been a direct hit, because Hugh simply disappeared. One moment he was there, firing wildly at the planes, the next there was a flash, some smoke, and he was gone. I guess he was right—it was personal and one of the bombs was aimed at him.

Bob and I struggled on and were almost at the olive grove when the shell exploded beside us. A piece of shrapnel caught Bob in the shoulder and something, a rock, I think, or maybe just a hard clod of earth, *hit me a stunning blow in the side, knocking all the air out of me. It took me a long time to get my breath back and my ribs hurt dreadfully, but there was no blood, so I figured I was probably all right. I worked my way to Bob, who was sitting, cradling his arm with blood soaking out of his wound. I helped him to his feet, and we stumbled into the trees.*

The first men we met tried to help us, but I told them to go back and get Tiny. I sat Bob by a tree and patched up his wound as best I could. Then I collapsed beside him.

There weren't many men left in the fields, not live ones anyway. Here and there, figures staggered along and wounded tried to crawl toward us between the inert bodies. The shelling had stopped, but I could see figures among the houses, picking off the wounded in the open with their rifles.

The two men I had sent for Tiny returned alone. "He's just out there," I said, pointing. "He's a big man. You can't miss him."

One of the men shook his head. "We found him, all right," he said, "but he's stone dead. Hole in his back I could put my fist in."

"You're wrong," I shouted. "Go back and get him."

The men simply shook their heads and wandered off. I tried to stand, but the pain in my chest made me gasp and collapse to the ground. Worse than that was the weight of all my dead friends, so heavy that it seemed it was pushing me down into the earth itself. Bob and I sat and wept openly beneath the olive tree.

Eventually, we rose and found our way to this aid station. I must try and sleep now. I cannot write more.

FIFTEEN

I turned the page in the journal, but the next one was blank. Laia was leaning against me, her head on my shoulder, crying softly. I put my arm around her shoulder and hugged her.

"All of them," she said softly. "It's tragic."

I stared down the overgrown street of ruins. It *was* tragic. More so than I could imagine. How could so much enthusiasm and hope have turned into so much disaster? How did my grandfather keep going through all of the horror happening around him? I'd complained about the uncomfortable scooter and the heat when I'd been traveling in absolute safety with a beautiful girl by my side. Could I have done what he did?

So the mystery was solved. The hole in Grandfather's young life, the passion that he still remembered as an old man, were explained. I had learned what I had come for, but that was nothing. I had learned so much more—about war, about how complicated life can be.

The phone in my pocket vibrated, but I ignored it. It was probably just DJ telling me he'd made it to the top of his mountain and how wonderful it all was. What did he know about struggles like the one Grandfather had been through?

Almost immediately, I felt guilty. It wasn't DJ's fault he'd been given a mountain to climb and just because I'd read Grandfather's journal and he hadn't didn't make me special in any way. Gently, so as not to disturb Laia, I reached into my pocket and extracted my phone. It *was* a text from DJ, but not what I expected.

It's over. I couldn't do it. Things happened.

Over! Couldn't do it! What had happened? Had dive-bombers attacked him on the mountain?

Suddenly I was angry. "You can't give up," I said out loud, lifting my arm from around Laia. She sat up and looked at my phone.

W@ u mean couldn't do it? Break your neck? I texted back.

"What's happening?" Laia asked.

"It's my twin brother, DJ. He's giving up."

"Giving up what? I didn't know you had a twin brother."

"I do," I said. My phone vibrated, and DJ's reply appeared.

Three of the people in our party got acute mountain sickness and had to be taken down the mountain. All the guides and porters except one had to go down.

How close r u 2 top? I typed.

"Where is he?" Laia asked.

"Halfway up Kilimanjaro in Tanzania," I replied. "I have a twin brother and five cousins. Grandfather gave us all tasks in his will."

Another text came in.

Thirteen hundred meters. Six hours. I can see it, but I was told by the guide not to go, that I couldn't go up.

I stared at the screen. This was so not DJ. He'd always been the one that did things, made things happen. As far as I knew, he'd never failed at anything in his life. Angrily, I texted back, If u can c it, u can do it. Just go to the top.

"He can't do it?" Laia said.

"Yes, he can," I said. "He always has. He's the strong one." I felt anger rising again.

I began texting. I forgot the protocol and the abbreviations, I just typed like I was talking to him. It took me three texts to send it all.

Just because someone says you can't do something doesn't mean you can't. Grandfather was exhausted and terrified. His friends were being killed all around him, but he kept going because he believed in something. It was a long time ago and that something failed, but he kept going as long as he could.

I hesitated, wondering what to say next. Had I gone too far? My phone pinged.

I'm tired. I'm sick. I don't think I can do it. I'm so sorry.

My anger surged up once more. What did he mean he couldn't do it? This was DJ talking. He was my big brother. My fingers flew over the keypad.

Don't be sorry. Go through the tired. Go through the pain. Believe you can do it. Try and you can't fail. You're as good as Grandfather. I believe in you. KUTGW bro. Grandfather's waiting at the top. KIT.

As soon as I sent the text, I felt embarrassed. It was so emotional. What would DJ think? More importantly, what would Laia think? I glanced at her. She was staring at the blank screen. She must think I'm such a nerd.

The screen lit up.

I'll try, for Grandpa and for you, bro. T4BU.

I smiled. I never thought he knew stuff like the shortcut for *Thanks for being you*.

"That was nice." Laia was looking at me.

"Really? You didn't think it was sappy?"

"Of course not. You persuaded your brother not to give up, just like your grandfather persuaded Bob to keep going. I'm proud of you. And I'm very glad your grandfather gave you this task." Laia leaned over and kissed me on the cheek.

I felt my face burning and fumbled to put my phone away. The journal slipped out of my hand and fell open at the last page. It was covered with my grandfather's small, neat handwriting.

"He wrote something else," I said. I picked up the book and thumbed through the last few pages. Several were blank after the battle, but Grandfather had written something on the last page. Laia and I huddled together over the notebook, enthralled by the final entry.

SEPTEMBER 8

It's been six weeks since I last scrawled my thoughts in these pages. After the battle, I was certain I would never write again. What was already there was so painful, how could I ever say anything worthwhile? But today I am in such a turmoil of conflicting emotions that I have to write something down.

After Gandesa, I thought the change that began when I crossed the mountains into Spain was complete, that the friends I had made and lost, the horrors I had seen, the tragedy I had been a part of, had molded me into a new person and that is who I would be. The last six weeks have proved simply that we can never be certain of anything.

Bob and I were shuffled back to Barcelona. It took five days, most of which we spent either lying ignored on the cold ground or rattling painfully somewhere in a truck or railway carriage surrounded by the stench and screams of those much worse off than ourselves.

A doctor in Tarragona removed the shrapnel from Bob's shoulder and painfully prodded my ribs before saying that there was nothing he could do. I have tried not to move my ribs, but it is hard not to breathe. However, the pain has pretty much gone and I think they have healed well. Not having a broken bone, Bob's wound healed much faster.

As we healed, we both assumed that we would return to the war eventually, but that is not to be. The battle has not gone well. The fighting continues, but we never took Gandesa and we have been steadily forced back. The Fascists have too many tanks, planes, guns and soldiers.

Rumors are flying around that the International Brigades are to be sent home. I think the rumors are true and that is why Bob and I are to be repatriated tomorrow. That is the cause of my conflicting emotions. I want to go home—I've had more than enough of war—but I also want to stay here. I have fallen in love.

Maria, the nurse I could not get out of my mind, was at the hospital in Barcelona when I returned and *was as happy to see me as I was her. Since then we have barely been out of each other's company. Her family has given me a bed in their house, and I have helped at the hospital, as much as my ribs allowed.*

In our spare moments between work and sheltering from the continuing bombing raids, we have walked the streets of this wonderful, damaged city. We have strolled through the parks and gardens and climbed the hill of Montjuïc. Maria has shown me the ancient cathedral and the tomb of Barcelona's favorite saint, Eulalia. We have walked the narrow dark alleys of the Gothic Quarter, eaten at whatever tiny places we have come upon and talked with the people struggling to survive and afraid of the coming Fascist darkness. If I live to be one hundred, I don't think I shall ever find another place so beautiful, friendly and alive— or so doomed.

My ribs healed on their own, but that was only my body. My mind as I left Gandesa was a mess. My nights were plagued by nightmares in which Tiny, Hugh and the others came back to haunt me, and my days were filled with shadowy thoughts of hopelessness and death. It felt as if I could never climb back out from that black pit.

Maria, with her love and patience, has brought me back. She has shown me that, despite everything, there is still good in the world. It is a lesson I will never forget, and I shall cherish every moment of happiness that I am given. But why must the cost of that lesson be so unbearably high?

If I had one wish, it would be to stay here forever with Maria or to take her somewhere else that is safe. Her wish is the same, but it is not possible. The war is lost and the Fascists will march down the Ramblas soon. Any foreigners who fought for the Republic will not last long after that. I can go because I am Canadian. Maria must stay because she is Spanish and the border is closed.

It is so unfair. So cruel to find love and lose it.

But I shall come back. I will leave my suitcase with all the pitiful possessions I have collected here, including this book. I will give them to Maria and pray that one day I will be able to return and collect them. Until then, these twelve weeks, this part of my life, the most important part until now and, I suspect, the most important part ever, will remain Maria's and my secret.

SIXTEEN

That was it, all there was. I thumbed through every other page in the journal, but they were blank.

"So your grandfather and my great-grandmother fell in love," Laia said quietly. "I suspected as much, but to see him declare his love on the page is different. Why did he never come back?"

"He did, once. His plane crashed in France during the war and he was sent through Spain to escape, but he was on the run. After the war, as long as Franco was alive and dictator of Spain, he couldn't return, but after that…? It was a different world after the Second World War. He got married, had kids."

"I wonder if he still loved Maria?"

"I don't know. Is it possible to love two people? He loved my grandmother very much and built a wonderful life for his family in Canada. Maybe he assumed that Maria had done the same in Spain and convinced himself that she had forgotten him."

"She never did." Laia smiled sadly. "When Barcelona fell, she fled with tens of thousands of other refugees to the camps in France. When the Nazi's invaded France, she went into hiding. She told me once that she did some work for the Resistance. After the war, she came back. They were hard times, but her parents had managed to keep the house, and she moved in with them. She lived there the rest of her life."

"She never married?"

"That's something I've thought about a lot," Laia said. "My grandmother was Maria's only child and she was born out of wedlock. That is a serious difficulty in Catholic Spain, but the times were chaotic and there were many young widows with children after the war."

I nodded, thinking about how hard life must have been for Maria and the other refugees in those days. But Laia hadn't finished telling me things.

"My grandmother was born during the war in France."

"It must have been tough with a new baby." Then a thought exploded in my mind. "When was your grandmother born?"

"I know what you are wondering, but your grandfather is not my great-grandfather. We're not related. My grandmother was born in 1944, near the end of the war."

I laughed. "At Grandfather's will reading, my five cousins and I discovered that we had a seventh cousin that no one knew about. I don't think I could handle finding out we were related, even though it would be like half cousins, a bunch removed."

"You don't want to be related to me?" Laia asked with a mischievous grin.

"I didn't mean it that way," I said.

"Of course," Laia went on, her smile broadening, "there were no paper records during the war. We only have Maria's word that my grandmother was born in 1944 and not 1939."

"Stop teasing me," I said, returning her smile. "I don't want to be your relative. I'd rather be your…friend."

I felt my face burning as I realized what I'd just said. "I mean…" I began, but Laia silenced me with a gentle touch on my cheek.

"I would like us to be friends as well," she said. "How long are you going to stay in Spain?"

"I have a ticket back in a couple of weeks."

"That gives us time, and you have got used to our scooters." Laia laughed and I grinned back stupidly. "We can visit my grandmother and I can show you Barcelona. Maybe we can even visit our famous beaches."

My heart was pounding. I was happier than I had ever been. I had discovered Grandfather's past and retraced his footsteps. Like him, I had found an amazing girl in Barcelona. Unlike him, I wasn't going to let her go.

"That would be fantastic," I said through a smile that hurt my cheeks. "I would love to discover Barcelona and visit some beaches. I know some people at the Hotel Miramar in Lloret de Mar. I'm sure they'd love to meet you."

ACKNOWLEDGMENTS

Thanks to Eric Walters for the idea and for his drive in getting six other writers heading in the same direction; to Andrew Wooldridge for seeing the potential in the idea and providing the platform for us to tell our stories; and to Sarah Harvey for making sure our stories mesh and that we're all on the same page.

Born in Edinburgh, Scotland, JOHN WILSON grew up on the Isle of Skye and outside Glasgow without the slightest idea that he would ever write books. John is addicted to history and firmly believes that the past must have been just as exciting, confusing and complex to those who lived through it as our world is to us. Every one of his twenty-five novels and nine nonfiction books for kids, teens and adults deals with the past. John lives in Lantzville, British Columbia. For more information, visit www.johnwilsonauthor.com.

SEVEN
THE SERIES

7 GRANDSONS
7 JOURNEYS
7 AUTHORS
1 AMAZING SERIES